THE GOOSE GIRL
OF ERISKA

THE GOOSE GIRL OF ERISKA

AND OTHER SCOTTISH STORIES

Anna Blair

RICHARD DREW PUBLISHING
GLASGOW

First published 1989 by
Richard Drew Publishing Ltd
6 Clairmont Gardens
Glasgow G3 7LW
Scotland

British Library Cataloguing in Publication Data

Blair, Anna
   The Goose Girl of Eriska: and other Scottish tales
   I. Title
   823′.914[F]

   ISBN 0-86267-244-9

Designed by James W. Murray

Set in Century Old Style by Swains (Glasgow) Ltd,
Printed and bound by Cox and Wyman Ltd., Reading

♨ ♨ ♨ ♨ ♨ ♨ ♨

For Valerie and Lindsey
With Love

tales from
Old Scotland
to
New England

♨ ♨ ♨ ♨ ♨ ♨ ♨

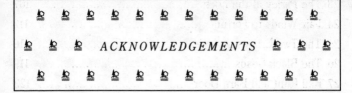

ACKNOWLEDGEMENTS

To all those who have helped me with this book I offer my thanks. I am indebted first to my husband for wise criticism and encouragement: to Mrs Edith Dykes and Mr H.G.A. Anderson for secretarial assistance and advice: to librarians who have been unfailingly helpful: and to those who retold to me local tales known to them since childhood.

I am grateful too, to the Publisher and his staff for attention and good counsel at every stage of the work.

A.B.

There is always a dilemma in tackling a book of this kind since many of the tales come, during the research, not as whole stories from one source-place but as scraps and references from perhaps four or five different areas. The folklore scholar would list, sift and annotate . . . setting out strictly and precisely what part of a tale comes from where, adding and subtracting nothing.

The story-teller, on the other hand, having researched with similar care considers the material and produces what he thinks is the most rounded tale from the jigsaw of information and sets it in the likeliest place. There should be integrity and authenticity in both approaches and the collector of these tales makes no apology that the book contains the latter, 'once-upon-a-time' type stories.

There are forty tales here, varying from the romantic to the fey, the tragic to the historical, with a leavening of the humorous and down-to-earth. Another aspect of selection has been to represent as many areas of Scotland as possible. This collection is drawn from North, South, East and West, the islands, the highlands and the lowlands, and is aimed at everyone and anyone for whom a story about this or that town or village enriches a visit there.

Anna Blair

O nce upon a time in the days long before they laughed at the notion of Little People, there lived on the tiny beautiful Hebridean island of Eriska a lonely young girl. She tended her father's geese on the machair by the flat shore near their simple home, which stood by itself some way from any of the other cottages. Shy by nature, she did not seek out the fisher lads or lasses who lived elsewhere on Eriska but preferred the quiet shoreland and the lap of water, the cluster of comical white geese round her skirts and bare feet, and the soft colours of sea-thrift and rocket spread across the sand. There, surrounded by silence save for the friendly cackle of the geese, she would croon softly in her sweet low voice that was true and clear as a bell, and that no one but herself had ever heard.

There could be a gentle moan in it like the wind in the sedge, or the quick outpouring of notes like she heard from a skylark, or sometimes a cooshing as of doves, maybe even the sighing sound the sea made in a conch shell. But never a real word did she sing. For she had never in her life heard anyone singing songs with lines in them to make sense or tell a story.

Then, on one of those still island mornings that made her feel that the world was newborn, the goose-girl was sure that she heard voices. But there was no one but herself the length or breadth of the beach. She walked slowly to and fro and found she was hearing the sound most clearly each time that she passed a particular mound of sand. She sat down beside it. Sure enough. She put her ear to the hummock and listened. Oh yes, there was singing from inside . . . Little People! She knew about them and the malices they did, unseen, at night . . . and sometimes, to be fair, the kindnesses. But she had never seen or heard them . . . until now. Their singing was not the mouth-music croon-songs that she sang herself. It had words, real words. She listened, clamped like a limpet to the mound until she made out every one . . .

over and over. She walked away, not to disturb them, and softly tried out this song-with-words in her own voice. It was a beautiful tune to a sad tale of black nights, white hearts and wild seas, of forlorn love left behind, but then of a moonlit pathway back to the dear one. Again and again she sang her love-song that day as she followed the geese, exulting in the match of sense to sound, with ro-van-oes and ro-van-i's that echoed through the refrain.

In the next few days she lingered by the throbbing mound to hear and learn new melodies with different words. And soon there wasn't a happier lass in all the islands than the goose-girl with her repertoire of elfin songs. Alone all day with none to heed or laugh at her, she sang as she wandered and began, by and by, to dream of a love that would make such songs for her.

One day as she lilted along the shore a lad from a croft on the hill, came up through the dunes behind the machair, to set his creels while the tide was out. He never forgot his first sight and hearing of the plain-dressed girl on the sand-flats, with her white geese, her beautiful hair and the clear singing that came from her as she tended the birds.

Soon he was walking with her there, part of every day, and taking her to ceilidhs and peat-fire nights among other friendly islanders. There she sang shyly to them the songs she had learned of the Little People. They were charmed by the lullabies, the children's rounds, the little sagas and the strange death dirges. But the favourite of them all was the love-lilt the Eriska goose-girl had heard that first morning from the mound. Soon the whole island was singing it, fisher-lads to their girls, croft-lads to milkmaids, mothers to bairns. Visiting packmen took it to other islands and girls sang it as they leaned over rock pools, hoping to see a true-love's face reflected there.

They say that for a time the Little People were angry to hear their songs echoing round the islands, but that, later, when they saw how happy these ordinary folk were in their singing, they were really quite well pleased. And after the three-day-long wedding that summertime of the crofter-lad and the goose-girl they never did another mischief to anyone on Eriska.

The story they tell in Edinburgh of Will Gunn, begins some-where up in the Highlands, the wilderness that to city folk in the late years of the 1700s was a misty, mysterious world apart, with inhabitants of strange appearance and custom. They say that, as a small boy, Will had stood at the graveside of his parents, both dead of a smit that had raked their glen, that they were buried without dignity, sharing a paupers' grave and that young Will had made a fierce vow that day to be kisted and laid decently to rest when his own time came.

And so, when he was old enough and had served his time as foster-son to kindly but impoverished kinsfolk, doing his small bit on sour croft land that barely kept them all, he set out to walk to Edinburgh where he would seek, if not his fortune, at least his salvation from shame.

There was an air of new beginnings and fresh ventures abroad, an upsurge of prosperity and the rising of the New Town, when Will reached the city in the early days of the year 1800. He was a strange figure with his red hair and the ancient, ill-fitting clothes, pressed on him by home well-wishers. On his long tramp he had slept behind dykes and in barns, and so a pile of straw in a shed at the back of an ale-house near the Grassmarket seemed compara-tively comfortable as a lodging. For that he gave the hostler an hour's work of a morning, sweeping the yard, and changing full for empty barrels in the inn itself.

Will was a God-fearing man, regular in his attendance at wor-ship, but his faith was not of the brand that made him sit back and wait for the Lord to provide, without his own assistance. He tramped the booths and alleys of the city looking for work, but since he habitually wore his entire wardrobe consisting of two sets of clothes (which he changed occasionally from inner to outer layer to give them an airing) he was not a prepossessing sight to prospective employers. Two or three weeks went by without an earned penny, and he existed therefore only on half pies, dregs from ale-house jugs and the occasional bawbee tossed to him as if he was a beggar. His Highland pride resented the coins and he swept the yard with extra smeddum to tell himself he was earning them.

But the wild appearance served him well enough in the end for there were echoes about him of John the Baptist and he was hired by the preacher at a meeting-hall to sell religious tracts round streets and markets.

He trudged the High Street vennels and wynds touting his wares. He was reviled by hearty topers and welcomed by maudlin' ones who wanted to do better. He winked at cheeky callants whose tormenting was unmalicious, and cuffed the ears of unpleasant bullies. Douce little ladies scurrying up and down the Cowgate bought and read his tracts, and sometimes a minister would lay a hand of blessing on his shoulder for his work.

His patch was wherever he wanted it to be and in time he even ventured over to the New Town. But best of all he liked to wander up to the south by Bruntsfield, where he was nearer to the moors and hills that minded him of home. It was a treat he did not allow himself too often, and only when he had had a fair morning's trade, for there was little selling of pamphlets to be done there.

When he wasn't lifting his eyes to the Braid and Pentland hills he took to enjoying another spectacle. There was a course set out at Bruntsfield where merchants who no longer had to scrabble in the market place, and other men of leisure, diverted themselves playing at the game he had heard cried gowf or goff. Will would stand fascinated while they took sticks and struck their balls between one small flag and another. There was a wild game in his home glen, but maybe twenty men there swarmed after one ball while here each player had his own.

He became a kenspeckle figure round the edges of the course and was soon on bonnet-lifting terms with most of the regulars. There was one shilpit wee lawyer who had always been very civil to Will, used his name to him too . . . and when he missed the man on the links for a week or two, he enquired after him of the goff-stick maker.

'He's chesty y'ken . . . confined abed w'it the now.' When Will next saw the lawyer, he was sorry to notice him peching about the course overburdened by the long bag he had slung on his shoulder to carry his clubs. He raised a weary hand to Will.

'It's sore short o' breath you are, lawyer. Could I be cadging that bag for you, sir?'

'I would be obliged to you, Will Gunn, if you'll tak' a sixpence for the carryin'.'

Will put the rest of his tracts into his pouch, lifted the golf bag off the narrow shoulder and had a glorious hour marching behind him round the course.

A time or two more, by arrangement with the lawyer, and the chapman had learned to stand well behind the player at each stroke, to keep quiet, to attend to the flag, clean the ball and anticipate which club his patron would need.

In another month he was answering to the name of 'Willie the Caddie' and cadging for half-a-dozen others; and in two, he felt he could set his own fee at a shilling an hour. He was invigorated by the air out of the city and when he found in the Canongate one morning another fortune-seeker come from the country, he gave up the tract-selling to him, and turned his talents full-time to carrying bags at Bruntsfield, as the first recorded golf caddie.

Through his friend the club-maker, he fell in with a gardener on one of the small estates nearby, who had a spare attic room with a bed, a table, a chair and a fire, which Will was able to rent at a reasonable rate. He rooted through his clothes and kept only the best of the two sets, then he bought a new sark and trousers and began to live civilised . . . and to put by his small savings week by week.

Maybe every second year, when he had a little put by, he disappeared to the Highlands again, to take a pound or two and maybe a bonnie head-shawl to the kinsfolk there that he never forgot, and to relish the clean mountain and glen air that even Bruntsfield could never match.

'Will's a gentleman now in Edinburgh town . . . friends with baillies and merchants and such . . . and making his fortune,' his aunt would tell neighbours proudly, secure in the knowledge that, unlike her departed sister, she would have a grand wake and funeral when the time came.

It was no fortune Will was making, for saving was slow work alongside offerings to his family, his rent and food and the douce clothes he needed to be respectable on the greens. A lifetime it took him, before he counted out his shillings and found at last that there was enough to cover the most honourable of burials. He was creaking now with rheumatics, but there was just enough ease left in the joints for the last tramp home. He made a final round at Bruntsfield with each of his gentlemen, had a last crack with the club-maker, paid up his rent to the gardener, and limped away into the hills, enough in his pocket to live modestly on the family croft, to have a grand sturdy coffin with his name on it, and as well as that, two or three serving-rounds of usque and cake for his friends to give him a good send-off.

LLOYD GEORGE
AND THE TURRIFF COW

There was a deal of mumping and grumping when the Welsh wizard first thought of taking away from old age, unemployment and poverty, the dread of work-house or vagrancy. Some said it was a step towards a new small dignity for the needy; but more saw it as a licence for sloth and thriftlessness, a foolish measure boding future ill, not only for the radical party that promoted it, but for the moral fibre of the nation. Not to mention the tax it was on their own pockets.

The Commons was in an uproar, the Lords had gentlemanly barneys and it was said that King George himself was much exercised as to the wisdom of his stubborn Liberal ministers.

If there was consternation in high places, that was nothing to the reception the new measure had in Buchan. In the ordinary way the folk there were never sure exactly what was what, about White Papers and Bills, Acts, Divisions and such like, and it was generally only when the outcome of the huffing and puffing in Westminster reached reality, through Post Offices or Police Station in the likes of Turriff, that the thing, whatever it was, was understood and judged good or bad, foolishness or sense.

The Insurance plan with its wee stamps that farmers with orra-loons and milking-quines, had to stick on daft-like squares on a card, was more quickly understood by Buchan folk. Men who usually clenched pipes in their teeth and only grunted at passing neighbours or nodded to each other at the Kirk on Sundays, would spend five minutes or more at a farm gate over the sinful iniquity of it all.

In the end, most were ready to damn it and pay up, but Paterson-Lendrum was a man with the temerity of his convictions.

'Awa' wi' you, man,' he said when his ploughman presented the farmer with a crisp new card for stamping. 'I'll see thon Lloyd George burn first!'

And Robert Paterson flatly refused then, and in the weeks and months following, to be ordered into not only paying his employees the wage they'd agreed at the feeing fair but giving Lloyd George a cut forbye.

'No' this week, nor any ither,' he said firmly, when more pliable farmers questioned his good sense.

'I'm as agin it as yoursel', Lendrum, but you canna just ignore what's the law.'

'Aye, watch me!' retorted Paterson and, opening a gate to lead in his cows for milking, whacked Buttercup's haunches with unaccustomed venom.

Even his sensible wife tried to wheedle him to paying, saying she thought changes were the way of the world.

'It's not a' "pay"; mind there's them as "gets".' And she told him she'd just heard that Beenie Dewar was to draw a nice wee pension for her old mother.

'Best just buy the stamps,' she urged. Nothing moved Paterson.

But if the farmer's dues were not be forthcoming in cash, an officious wee clerk from the new department ordered the confiscation of some other piece of his property.

'The man's a fool,' raged Robert Paterson. 'He'll no can carry off my carts or milk-cans, nor the Mistress's piano.' And then he laughed at the thought of a posse of pen-pushers breaking in and carrying off his gear.

They had a busy morning in the Aberdeen office doing sums and balancing overdue stamps against the stock at Lendrum and then, when their calculations were complete. . . .

'Did they no' just come up by, calm-as-you-please, when I was in the far field, and lead awa' my best white coo?' he exploded to a shocked circle in the inn that night.

Next day there was an even more shocking event, for notices appeared on posts and gates and shop windows that the beast was to be auctioned off to the highest bidder, in Turriff Town Square.

There were a few sour chiels that said Rob Paterson had brought it on himself, who wiped the froth from their mouths and slammed down their beer jars with the air of men who had seen it all coming. But there were others who saw him as a brave, thrawn champion of what they sneakingly believed themselves, . . . a man not to be cheated of a fine beast. There was a muttering among them against any local man that would be tempted to buy the cow.

So there was a rare turnout for the auction and, from the safe cover of the crowd, less brave men than Robert Paterson drummed up the courage to throw showers of eggs and harmless turves at the auctioneer's tweed bunnet, and one reckless loon took advantage of the hullarackit to unhitch the cow and lead her lumbering out of the square where she ran amok along the street.

There was no sale for the white cow in Turriff that day. She was caught later by the auctioneer's man when her rump got stuck in a lane between two shops.

Eventually she was sent out of harm's way and sold at the Aberdeen market.

But the Turra-Buchan farmers were better organised now, declaring a small war on officialdom. Their headquarters was the inn and when Tam Glennie reported back from Aberdeen the name and farm of the cow's buyer, he ended his spiel by throwing a pound note on the counter and challenging the rest to match it. Next day a negotiating team was sent down Inverurie way to locate and buy back the white cow.

Turriff townsfolk left off their regular chores that day and gathered at street corners, outside the station and in the town square. Farms were left with only a few minders, and half-day holiday was called for any who 'blawed or drummed' in the Turriff brass band. When the puzzled beast arrived home that afternoon the band struck up 'Jock o' Hazeldean' and she was led in triumph through the town. Then the whole procession made three or four rounds of the square, cheered by near four thousand supporters, some of them holding banners miscalling that same 'George Lloyd' they would all have good cause to bless before their lives were done.

After this performance the cow was presented back to Paterson-Lendrum and in due course was contentedly swinging her rear-end into the milking-shed again, as if nothing had ever happened.

Robert Paterson considered he'd had a prime victory, and when he and Mistress Paterson sat down to their tea that night he was ready for his next week's defiance over the stamps.

'Na, na, Rob Paterson, you'll hae to pay your dues now. You've had your fling and you canna hae your freens to bail y'oot again.' Rob opened his mouth, then shut it again and went out to the byre.

Next day he turned the whole matter over to his sensible wife to look after, stamp-cards, leaflets and threatening letters. And so Robert Paterson-Lendrum himself never did stick stamps on an Insurance card.

Whether it was after her adventure or just a seasonal improvement in the animal's condition, the Lendrum milkmaid was said to have reported that the white cow, never the best of milkers, was yielding something-marvellous, that her milk was rich and creamy and 'fair sang as it scooshed into the pail'.

Later they made rhymes about the Turra Coo, songs that folk-singers put on records; and the grand fiddler, Scott Skinner, wrote a rousing tune that men whistle to this day, three quarters of a century after the famous white cow was laid to rest in the fullness of time, with a fine gravestone over her bones.

The battle of Langside was over. Mary, Queen of Scots had fled across the Solway to begin her long imprisonment in England and her infant son had been proclaimed King James VI. The flighty, foolish, tragic reign was over and the young King's Regent and Council were trying to bring their version of stability back to Scotland. If Mary had been dead, that worthy aim might have been more quickly and smoothly achieved. But Mary was very much alive and there was still a core of her supporters ready to intrigue and prepare to bring her back again.

There were two fortresses still fiercely and loyally held for what some called the Queen's Party. One was Edinburgh Castle itself and the other the stout stronghold of Dumbarton under Lord Fleming, towards which Mary had been heading when she was stopped in her tracks at Langside.

Dumbarton Castle was said to be well-nigh impregnable and so long as the Queen lived, the Regent and his party saw it as a smouldering coal ready to flare up if there should be an uprising for Mary's restoration. Situated as it was in the Firth of Clyde it could be a dangerous foothold too, for an invasion from the south, from Ireland or by an army from France. As the months wore on after the Queen's flight, it became an outrage not to be tholed, that one of the greatest fortresses in the land should be held by the supporters of a discredited regime.

Parleys were held, charts and maps drawn up, of the Castle, its rock-plinth, its two humps and the short peninsula on which it stands. Names were put forward of various intrepid soldiers who could best mount an assault. The leet narrowed to those who were most familiar with the west of Scotland, and then to a handful of experienced officers who knew the Clyde river and the contours of land around Dumbarton.

Of those few stalwarts there was one man with not only the

qualifications but clutch of reasons for wanting to lead that assault.

Not many of his contemporaries had been devoted to Henry Stewart, Lord Darnley, certainly not his wife after the first week or two of marriage. But one who did have a loyal regard and even affection for him was Tom Craufurd, sometime soldier, erstwhile gentleman-at-court to Darnley and, after his master's death, soldier and officer again as Captain Thomas Craufurd. His lands were at Jordanhill, an estate no more than a dozen miles from Dumbarton Castle.

In the early days of his appointment at court Tom Craufurd had been honoured to serve the handsome couple who were Queen and King of Scots and distressed to see the widening breach between them. His family had for generations served the Lennox tree of which Henry was a sprig, and so he edged in his allegiance towards the nineteen-year-old Darnley, foolish, weak (some said vicious) though he was. And finally in the youth's jealous confusion and bewilderment over his wife's capricious tastes and friendships, Craufurd became his closest friend and adviser. He was at the young man's side when he went a-hunting, he tried to curb him when he went a-drinking and to warn him against rash amorous adventures. He sat with him of an evening when Mary was enjoying the more sophisticated pleasures that bored her husband. Whether Thomas Craufurd was privy to the truth about David Rizzio's violent end, tradition does not tell.

Later Craufurd nursed Darnley faithfully through the pox in Glasgow and was witness to Mary's pleading there with him to come back to Edinburgh and be reconciled with her. Craufurd watched and listened with distaste, and the suspicion that it was as her prisoner and not her mate that Mary desired her husband, and he vainly urged the invalid not to go. But the King made his last naive ride to Kirk o' Field.

Now, it was four years since Darnley's death by strangling and explosion, and many who had despised him in life as unstable and unfit consort, now rosied him into no worse than a silly youth who had deserved scolding and taming, rather than murder. To Craufurd he was more. He was a martyr to Mary's infamy and Thomas would have joined any crusade to avenge him and help set his son James more firmly on the throne.

Another claim that the Captain had for leading the attempt on the Dumbarton garrison was that his anger with the Catholic Mary had turned him from the Church of his Craufurd forefathers. Whether he was a convinced Protestant or merely a man who saw how the land lay, he was now for the new Kirk, the new King and the new Establishment. A third reason was simply the military challenge of taking the dark Castle that brooded for Mary Stuart on his doorstep. But, over-riding all of those, the motive which drove Tom Craufurd was that, inside Dumbarton Castle, there skulked John Hamilton, Archbishop of St. Andrews, one of those most deeply implicated in the assassination of Darnley. Mary, if she was guilty, was already punished, Bothwell in prison, others disgraced or afraid and lying low, but Craufurd would have given his all to root out Hamilton and bring him to justice.

So that was Thomas Craufurd with his bevy of reasons for being in command to take Dumbarton Castle, and it was scarcely surprising that the choice of the Regent and of Darnley's family, the Lennoxes, fell on the Captain to lead the sortie.

Craufurd went at once to Glasgow, to his home at Jordanhill where he spent some weeks in meticulous preparation, planning and calculating. He rode back and forward along the shores of the Clyde by the hamlet scattered round the junction of the peninsula with the riverside, surveying from there the Castle on its rocky base. He chose a small army of men, handpicked for their daring, discipline and initiative, briefed them carefully and trained them at Jordanhill in the skills of ropes and scaling-ladders. And he found a scout. He had made enquiries and met secretly with a former castle-warden, one John Robertson who, from his years of service at the fortress knew every jut, cleft and blind access on the rock and every weakness in the castle wall. Bribed by Craufurd, or perhaps disenchanted with the Queen's cause, he put himself at the commander's disposal and was recruited as part of the vanguard. Three others were in that select band, among them an alert lad, younger than the rest, whose eagerness for the venture reminded Tom Craufurd of his own young self. His name was Angus Nimmo and he had a very particular reason for wanting to prove himself, which he let fall to no one during those days of preparation.

It was after sunset on a May evening of 1571 when a mist lay above the river, that the Captain made his approach along the north bank. He depended on surprise for success, and on the sense of security that the years of holding the Castle had given Fleming's garrison. There would be no loose-tongued clash reaching them from travellers, for Craufurd had sent out horsemen to round up and detain for an hour to two, any wayfarers abroad that evening.

The mist at Dumbarton was banking, conveniently heavy round the Castle itself but at the rock-base where the army would set its ladders, quite clear. At John Robertson's exact bidding the first ladder was raised against the base and the four leaders, with ropes looped round their shoulders, began to climb. But there was a sudden rasp, a scraping of iron on rock and the ladder slewed sideways across the face throwing the four to the ground. They were unhurt, and the silent army froze, as they waited for the dreaded sign that the echoing noise had disturbed the garrison. There was none.

Carefully the ladders were raised again and this time the iron craws caught fast in a crevice and held firm. The four with their ropes went up a second time to a broad ledge where Robertson pointed out an ash tree that had taken root, firm and deep. Lines were thrown round it, ready for more men to scramble up. The vanguard hauled their ladder towards them and planted it on the ledge, ready for the rest of the climb.

The three veterans started up, followed by young Nimmo. Next in line was Thomas Craufurd and below them an impatient but obedient army at various points on the ascent. The men were quietly exultant to have gone thus far without challenge and the Captain felt that his new Protestant God was surely on the side of his expedition.

But there were eighty fathoms still to go. Suddenly there was a choking sound from Angus Nimmo immediately in front of Craufurd. The boy clutched at the sides of the ladder knowing in his last conscious moments that one of the fits he was so desperate to overcome by putting to the test his own will and courage, had seized him. He lay vertically, brow, hips and knees against three rungs, clamped in a rigid spasm, obstructing all upward and downward movement of the others. From behind Craufurd heard the murmuring of the soldiers waiting to climb. They could not see the mishap and he dared not shout orders to wait. He tried to loosen the claw-like hold Nimmo had on the ladder, shuddering at the thought of having to pitch the boy to the rocks below. There was almost relief that the fingers were as if frozen to the wood.

But there was a castle to be won for the King. He pulled the rope from the young soldier's shoulder and lashed the unconcious body to the ladder. Then, gesticulating to those behind to go back to the ledge and the base, he himself slid quickly down to join them. Carefully, silently, they turned the ladder so that the rigid, roped body was now on the underside, firmed the ladder again by the iron-craws and started the climb yet again, assured that if Nimmo came out of his seizure he would be safe until he could be rescued.

Assured now of more men coming to join them the three in the first party moved on swiftly upwards to the top. An alert sentry's challenge and his warning to his fellows was muffled as they leapt on him and on two others scrambling to his help. Pressure from the invaders on a suspect part of the wall breached it and allowed a surge of Craufurd's soldiers to pour through, and the long defence of Dumbarton Castle was over. The King's soldiers swarmed like ants over the fort, flushing out the garrison and the families living there with them.

Lord Fleming, the governor, whether from panic or, more honourably, to fight for his Queen from some other vantage point, fled down a seaward cliff path, threw himself into a small boat and escaped into the river mist.

Four of the defenders were dead but the rest of the Castle community was quickly rounded up. Lady Fleming, unceremoniously left behind by her husband, was allowed to gather her jewellery and household treasures and given safe-conduct off the Rock. The French ambassador, an envoy between Mary's faction and her French in-laws was taken for questioning along with a few minor nobles, leading officers, a minstrel or two and a secretary.

But it was for none of those that Craufurd ransacked halls, ante-rooms and chambers in Dumbarton Castle that early May morning. He was stalking John Hamilton, arch-villain, murderer of Darnley. One after another he threw aside five or six men of similar build mistaking them for the Archbishop in the turmoil of shouting men and the drifting shroud of mist. And then at last in a downstairs orderly-room he found his quarry trying hastily to don a mail surtout over his night shirt.

Craufurd would fain have killed the holy-man murderer there and then but that might have made a martyr of him rather than a warning example. Instead he was taken prisoner to face proper trial.

The assault was over and Craufurd had finished his task cleanly. Another bastion for the exiled Queen had fallen without indiscriminate bloodshed. He had lost none of his own men and only a handful of defenders had died. There was no dallying over the retribution to the Archbishop. He was hurried to Stirling and within four days had faced the charge of murdering the young King, been convicted, gibbeted, drawn and quartered.

As some kind of amends or memorial to Darnley, the Governorship of Dumbarton went to the Lennox family. Thomas Craufurd himself enjoyed the favour of their patronage for the rest of his days, promoted during his soldiering years and elevated to be Provost of Glasgow when he retired to Jordanhill.

The bringer of near-failure to the whole enterprise, young Angus Nimmo who had recovered and been taken down from the parcel they had made of him on the scaling ladder, had been advised to come to terms with his disability and turn to less exciting labour than soldiering, some say as a forester on the Jordanhill estates.

Note: Dumbarton Castle has had a long history from Pictish times. As Dum Bretane (the fort of the Britons) it was said to have been the birthplace of St. Patrick before he was sold into captivity in Ireland. King Duncan and John Baliol knew it, William Wallace was a prisoner there, Robert the Bruce captured it as a stronghold, and it fell in turbulent times to the young James IV; still later to the French. But it is that well-documented feat of Thomas Craufurd's and the ladder incident that captures the imagination, and almost bring to an end Dumbarton's story as a fortress of war. There was a brief occupation by a party of Covenanters, but thereafter a calm fell on the old pile, and the next newsworthy mention of it is of the quiet visit of Dorothy Wordsworth and the recording of her pleasure in the view it afforded her of the beautiful Firth of Clyde.

THE RED DRESS

Long ago near the lovely sands of Carinish, North Uist, there lived a very vain woman whose dearest wish was, not to be kind or gentle or good, nor even to be beautiful with the beauty that shines through from a contented heart, but to possess a red dress. Perhaps that was because red was not a colour much seen in those parts, and for a very good reason. The women dyed their weavings from the plants they found on the moorland to the north-east. Lichen from rocks and boulders gave them saffrons and there were rich creams and greens from heather blossom, there was violet-blue to be steeped from vinca-periwinkle trailers, and autumn brown from brambles. They laughed and sang as they gathered leaves and flourish and were happy wearing the soft shades they so expertly rendered from their pickings. But red was denied them, because red came from the roots of the shore plants, tormentil and silverweed, that crept over the soft island sands. Its runners and roots meshed the loose surface, holding it firm against the wild winds from the Sound of Monach that would have laid it waste. The carpet made by the plants formed the machair the community depended on for the grazing of its cattle; and so, age-old island custom and unwritten law forbade the pulling up of their roots. Without that holding, wandering vegetation, the sand could be blown away in a single night and simple subsistence destroyed. None in living memory had dared to defy that law but all had heard-tell of the instant deaths, of mysterious disappearance of disobedient ancestors, and were warily respectful.

But it was a red dress, the only red dress on the island that Kate McAnnon craved, not cream nor nut-brown nor purple . . . but red.

When her husband first heard murmur from his wife that a handful or two of the weed and wild flowers from the machair would not be missed, he was angry and warned her sharply not to be foolish enough to dismiss the ancient island wisdom. But the more her wish seemed denied her, the more desirable the dress became and the more determined Kate was that the 'wisdom' was but an old wives' tale.

And so one night when her man was away at the fishing she slipped out of the house in the dark and had scrabbled up only a short stretch of the precious root . . . nowhere near enough to steep for a dress, or much damage the machair . . . when a sudden rush of wind whipped up the sea and swirled round her, as if she were the eye of a great storm.

Kate McAnnon was never seen in those parts again, but they say that the next evening the rosy northern aurora lights trailed like glowing curtains across the sky and that, along with the other awed islanders, her sorrowing husband guessed fine what she had been up to on the dark machair, the night before.

It was perhaps the same kind of torment that had wracked Macbeth in the days following Duncan's murder, that put him into the unwise paddy that begins this tale. His rage cast long shadows over the future for many a year and claimed Macbeth himself as its first victim.

A king needs a fitting castle and Macbeth was having one built at Dunsinane. The place rang with hammers and the sounds of stone being set on stone. Workmen swarmed inside and out, calling for materials to match their skills. Macbeth's once-fellow-nobleman, Macduff, Thane of Fife, was called upon to provide teams of oxen for their haulage and, when they were slow to come, Macbeth, sure of himself now only when he was drowning out his conscience by bawling orders, was furious.

'Faith, but I'll put a yoke on the Thane o' Fife's neck for treason. Mind, bring him here straightway he sets tardy foot at Dunsinane.'

Since the new king was more likely to put a blade than a wooden yoke to his neck, Macduff discreetly turned his men and beasts round, on hearing of the threat, making hastily for the south and the safety of Fife. Incensed, Macbeth ordered a party of cutthroats after him. But there was a short cut to the Fife thanedom, a pass near the Earn river known only to Macduff. King Macbeth's men lost the pursuit. Macduff escaped to England, found Malcolm the displaced heir and offered him his sword.

Macbeth did not have long to rant and bully after loyalty, or to savage those who did not give it. Led by Malcolm, the woods of Birnam marched on Dunsinane. As the battle started, Macduff cast aside his tree, came face to face with Macbeth and killed him.

Remembering his escape by the narrow Earn pass, and perhaps as a memorial to the wife and family the King had butchered in his absence in England, Macduff asked of the restored Malcolm to grant that the place should, from that time, mark the northern boundary of his Thanedom and be a place of refuge for his family. Malcolm did that and more; to the Law of Sanctuary for the Clan Macduff and all within nine degrees of kinship, he added the perpetual privilege that the clan should set succeeding kings on the Stone of Destiny for their crowning.

The Thane planted a great cross at the refuge spot on a plinth of freestone. Round it were fastened nine iron rings.

'Him as seeks safe keeping for fault, must grasp hold one of these hand rings and there declare his claim to sanctuary. Nine cows and a young colpindach must he give to the poor, and cleanse himself of his sin in the spring waters at the Nine Wells. Any who wantonly claims a ninth of kinship, falsely, will warrant instant death.'

Those were the conditions for sanctuary and for a time it was a holy place. Only men who truly repented their ill-deeds sought absolution there. But as the generations passed and that honest Macduff's descendants multiplied, many of them neglected the church confessional for the refuge, and some even planned their crimes in the knowledge that they had only to fly to Cross Macduff and perform the old ritual to escape the consequences.

There were Macduffs who looted and raped after skirmishes, some who fired houses during family feuds; there was even a maverick Macduff at eight removes from the direct line who wrecked and pillaged small merchant ships off the Fife East Neuk round the point of Tentmuir. All of those, and more, used the rings of Cross Macduff to forgive themselves their sins.

So for two centuries rogues among the Macduff tribe exploited the old dispensation and their fell deeds in those uncommunicative days were absorbed and lost in the mists along the Earn river, so that none further afield ever heard of them. There was no resentment from less privileged convicted neighbouring felons who only wished they had the same lucky touchstone in their families.

And then, in 1391, Sir Alexander Macduff had some trifling disagreement with Sir William, Laird of Spaldying, which could have been easily resolved by small appeal to Law. But Spaldying had been a minor thorn in Alexander's breeks in other matters equally trivial, a few disputed acres, the poaching away of an efficient steward, an invitation for Spaldying to dine with the new King, Robert III, which did not include Alexander. He brooded lightly for some months and then, chancing to pass the old Cross Macduff one day as he rode along by the Earn, he was first shocked at the idea that flashed into his irritated mind. And then intrigued. For the more he thought on the offer of the nine rings, the more he judged that a chill dip in the Nine Wells spring and nine-and-a-half head of cattle were small price to pay to be rid of his annoyance.

A few weeks later Sir William Spaldying was found dead beside his whinneying horse. Alexander did not trouble to conceal his blame, for he had ridden post-haste to the Cross, grasped the nearest ring and, reminding a few field-worker witnesses who were within earshot that he was a Macduff claiming his right, he set aside his cows for the needy and was ready to dip himself in the Nine Wells spring.

Since, for over two hundred years, there had been no public outcry over the use of the Cross Macduff, Alexander expected no more than a ripple of local admiration to follow. But by that year of 1391 there were more travellers, more itinerant dominies and market-mummers to carry tales across the country and, although King Robert III had a crippled body he was not too fragile to be roused by the injustice of a murdering man cocking a snook at his Royal Justiciary. He called the old tradition in question for the first time. But the law was the law, and Alexander had used it; and presently the king had other matters on his mind, for his young son and heir, James, had been taken captive to England. The Spaldying scandal was crowded out and became but yesterday's news, leaving Alexander privately gleeful over the whole adventure. It was not until thirty years later that there was another gamble with authority over the Cross Macduff, a crime that truly set the public by the ears.

Not far from Alexander's home-seat lived the baron Sir John Melville, harsh, brutal and the scourge of lesser men. He oppressed tenants and labourers, and had mere infants toiling on his furrows and in his mines. In his capacity as Sheriff too, so men said, he would as lief hang a man for petty theft as for murder. More lenient neighbouring landowners resented his tyranny over his workers and those who came before him for small infringements, and four of the lairds protested to the Regent Albany (for the young King James I was still a prisoner in England). Albany heard them out, but, in promising a word of warning to John Melville, he let fall an overhasty judgement on the offending laird.

'The man's an animal as should be boiled into a pot o' broth!'

One of the noble lairds, looser-tongued than the rest, repeated the Regent's rash words to the now-ageing Alexander of the Macduffs, who looked back nostalgically to his own youth, and chuckled.

'Yourself, Mather, Lariston and Pitarra y'say,' he mused. 'Guid men all . . . *and* all inside nine kinships wi' Macduff. You might well mak' use o' that.' And, as old men will, about old days and ways, he deaved his visitor with the ancient tale of his own derring-do.

The gossip went back to his friends. They may have been more just than the harsh Sheriff Melville, more loved by their underlings and by each other, but collectively they had a taste for the macabre, and grimly set about planning his retribution.

A few weeks later the four lairds arranged a small hunting party to Garvock Hill and, if the Sheriff John Melville was surprised to be invited to join it, he enjoyed the chase too much to decline. After an hour of cheerful riding on the lower slopes they wound their way towards the summit. There, before Melville could exclaim at the sight of two-three serving-men feeding a fire which cracked and leapt round a great cauldron, his four companions fell on him and bundled him into the boiling water.

'Broth ye, Sheriff Melville, as the guid Albany wid have ye be,' gloated Mather and, feeding each other's cruelty and quenching any misgivings, the rest agreed, as Melville's cries grew faint, that they were but doing the Regent a public service and ridding the country of a tyrant.

When their victim was safely dead, the righteous vigilantes leapt to their horses and rode pell-mell for Cross Macduff. They declared their deed, claimed immunity, and plunged themselves into the spring. Three dozen cows awaited later distribution to the poor and the farm lairds waited for a roar of approval from Regent Albany.

The Regent, however, was more sensitive to changing times and the shocked gossip of ordinary folk. But he was guiltily aware of his own part in the affair and judged that the old law of Macduff still held. Nevertheless, shortly afterwards, without relating his actions to the crime at the place people were now calling Sheriff's Pot, he deprived the lairds of wide stretches of land, demanded vast supplies of store and stock for the King's armies, and confiscated much of their family treasure.

When King James I came home at last, two years later, young, strong and wise, he heard tell of past abuses of royal mercy and quietly rescinded such ancient favours as Malcolm's at Cross Macduff, making Scotland gradually a juster land.

But even the King could not lay the ghost that flitted and moaned for generations round Garvock Hill after the pot-boiling there; the same spirit that haunted the free-stone cross in Strathearn; and made the nights of the four lairds a life-long misery of fear.

THE FUDDLED TALE
OF KIND KYTTOCK

The fey tale of the gude-wife they called Kind Kyttock has as many versions as there are tellers of it round Falkland way. But this is how the oldest inhabitant of a nearby hamlet had the story, half-a-century ago.

In her maiden years Kyttock had come from far away across the

Forth, south a league from Edinburgh, from the place they called Littil France (because some of the ladies Queen Mary had brought from the French court, lodged there).

In those days, when Kyttock came as bride to her man, who served at the palace as a falconer, she was a winsome, lively girl; a coquette, as was many a lass from Littil France who aped Queen Marie's demoiselles.

Her first tasks as new wife were to arrange her small home and to learn her big, slow man's whims and fancies, to observe the corners on him that, for comfort's sake she would have to smooth away. Then she bore his bairns . . . a girl and seven grand lads, all with their father's two side-quiffs of black hair. She buried three and steered the rest to man and womanhood, then wed them off with good tochers of linen and pewter plate. She scrubbed and cooked, stitched and stoked, she gave milk to her tabby cats, grew kails and curing herbs, and tended a few chickens in her bit-garden. She was first to chap a door when there was trouble and quick to offer passers-by refreshment. Yet even in all the busyness of her days, as she grew old and her back became bowed like a swee-hook, (near to the village bairns, she said, to hear their little secrets and give them marchpane sweetmeats) she was still the blithe, bonnie honest wench her man had married, with a complexion like the bloom on her garden plums and always a fresh lace cap, white as snow, on her head. And she was kind.

In fact she was that near to perfect that the good folks of Falkland, except perhaps for Nicol Moncrieff, were as sure as Kind Kyttock was herself, that the one failing she had would certainly not keep her from the blessings of Heaven when she died. She thought a lot about Heaven did the falconer's wife.

For Kyttock, it has to be said, had a great drouth for the ale-stoup. She could out-drink the menfolk at the inn then toddle back to her own kitchen and still have her man's sup on the table before he had left off talking at the vennel-end to Nicol Moncrieff, who tagled her man every night when their work was done, and kept him from his meat.

They say it's what a man or woman loves best, kills that body in the end. Well, Kyttock loved a lot of things forbye the ale . . . her man, her bairns and grand-bairns, her garden and her fellow-men. But if that saying is true the ale must have had a wee edge over the others, for it was at the close of a mellow afternoon among her michaelmas daisies and with an emptied keg at her side that Kyttock keeled over gently and went fearlessly to her Maker.

The dwam that she died in must still have been on her, for her mind (or was it her soul?) was in a rare old fuddle as she set out on the highway to Heaven. For she had a strange, queer dream that she strayed off that road to an elfin well, where there was only plain water to drink and never a sign-post to God. She dovered a while and then blinked herself awake, sure now that she was not dreaming, and saw a snail, yes, a snail, squeezing and stretching its way past her.

'Guid snail, ken ye the road to St. Peter's yett?' she asked.

'I'm makin' that way now. Best hurry after me.' She was not too fuddled to laugh.

'I'll keep up wi' you, gin you run a hunner times as fast.'

And they set off, he with his shell, she with her crooked back, humping along like echoes, until it grew dark and they had not yet reached the Gate. What they had reached though, was an ale-house on that Heavenly road, much like the one in Falkland. There the snail left her.

'Just a half-mile up the road the morn, and ye'll be there,' he instructed as he hunched away.

There was no great hunger on Kyttock, but her old dry thirst was there. That evening she drank deep of the inn's brew and, although hours meant nothing now, nor day nor night, in this world-beyond, she slept until what, in Falkland, would have been noon next day, and time to feed the cats.

She made haste now along to the pearly yett and, shamed a bit that she had lost her way yesterday, she jinked a moment behind a pillar then slipped in past Peter's back, that was uncannily like that of Nicol Moncrieff. The Good Lord saw her and laughed as he hadn't laughed since the night of the Sixth day when his creating work was done.

Heaven had looked down over all the years on Kyttock, her skills in house and garden, and at all her kind ways with neighbours; and she supposed that was why they made her under-hen-wife to Our Lady there.

For seven earthly years Kyttock lived a righteous life, for the ale in Heaven was sour and did not tempt her away from near-perfection; 'near' perfection, since there are those who say that, because of jouking past him that first day, she squabbled with St. Peter whenever they met. But since, except for a sharp word on occasion with Nicol Moncrieff, Kyttock had never quarrelled with anyone in Falkland, that was maybe Peter's blame.

And then one fateful day as she wandered near the Gate with the hens scratching round her feet, she caught a glimpse of the ale-house along the road, and of a sudden she was gripped by a terrible ache for a long cool draught. She forgot Our Lady's hens and her seven virtuous years, and again slipped past Peter and made to the inn. There she sat in the garden with the michaelmas daisies and two tabby cats at her feet, happily quenching her thirst.

And that was that. Peter was not to be caught a third time and sternly stopped her at the Gate when she came back that night, a little mist-eyed and unsteady. He cuffed her ears and sent her packing to the ale-house for all eternity.

There she took up something very like her old life in Falkland, cleaning, baking, sweeping, and pouring out pitchers of ale for passers-by; so that when one by one her friends and family joined her 'en route' (a phrase she still had from her days in Littil France) for Heaven, what with the chores, the purple daisies, the cats and the ale, she was never sure just *where* she was.

THE BROOCH OF LORNE

On a wild, dark night of 1286 King Alexander III fell from his horse over a Fife cliff and broke his neck. In the years following that tragedy the Scots first floundered for want of a strong heir and then squirmed under the weak vassal-king, John Balliol, selected for them by their dominating neighbour Edward I of England. Those were the days of risings and suppressions and the taking south of the ancient Stone of Destiny, of the infuriating demands and cruelties of Edward and of the brave, forlorn attempt by William Wallace to bring independence back to Scotland.

At last Balliol abandoned his unproud position and fled to the continent. Of the several claimants to the vacant crown two were eventually riddled out as main rival contenders. Those two were John Comyn the Red, and Robert Bruce. There were bitter words and blows between the two men which came to a climax with the killing of Comyn by Bruce before a Dumfries church altar. That act of sacrilege is part of the folk-heritage of Scotland.

After the death of Comyn, Bruce had himself crowned at Scone. Only the handful of friends who were present at that coronation recognised him as King. Many people had never heard of him. Others, perhaps ambitious themselves for the crown, would have been more than happy to see him dead. Nevertheless 'King Robert' was what he called himself as he went skirmishing about the countryside seeking support. Sometimes he was in hiding, sometimes defying his enemies in pitched battle, or in one-to-one challenge, winning and losing in equal measure.

Some months after his crowning Robert's small army suffered one of its defeats, at Methven. The straggle of escaping men, with Bruce riding at their head was dispirited and exhausted. But the King, anxious for their safety, was urging them on, to leave the Perthshire hills behind and reach refuge in Argyll.

But now the rashness and infamy of the Red Comyn incident

was about to come home to roost. Comyn's son-in-law, John Mac-Dougall of Lorne, had had revenge for that killing very much on his mind these last months. He had sent out spies to stalk Bruce and in July, after the fight at Methven, they reported his troop to be trudging wearily westward through Perthshire. This was just the word MacDougall had waited for, and he set out at once to confront this Bruce, who styled himself 'King Robert'.

The King and his party had reached the valley of Strathfillan and were now resting at Dalry near Tyndrum. Happed in a surtout-mantle fastened across his breast with a large studded silver brooch (which he had had in a gift of one of those present at his crowning), Robert lay awake, tense for an unchancy footfall or whinny. Towards dawn he heard both, suddenly close, MacDou-gall's troops were on them. The King's men, rudely wakened, grasped their weapons and stumbled to their feet.

That corner of the strath rang with the clash of blades and echoed the cries of wounded men and horses. There was a whirl-ing of axes, a rearing of animals and Bruce, through the melée, saw that the other force not only outnumbered his party, but was fresh and in better heart. Retreat and flight now was surely politic and might leave them alive to fight another day.

The King threw himself in front of his tired men, stretching out his huge broadsword in one hand, his axe in the other, making a span of nearly fourteen feet, to play for time for his force. Behind him, at his order, his men were scrambling away in individual escapes through woodland and scrub. Bruce threw aside three men, and now it was MacDougall himself who came face to face with the King.

'A truer fight is this, Robert Bruce,' growled the Chief, his long Lorne face eager for satisfaction as he lunged at Bruce's sword with a sturdy staff. 'Truer than striking dead a man in secret before his church altar . . . and that man my own wife's father . . . with more claim to Kingship than yourself.' A swingeing figure-of-eight with the staff and Bruce's weapons flew from his grip. Then the two were fighting on the ground, hand to hand, until Robert found his own short sword lying beside him within his grasp. MacDougall, now underneath him, was at the King's mercy.

But two of the Chief's men saw his danger and leapt in to pull Bruce off MacDougall and plunge their daggers into him. They clutched at the King's mantle but, now aware that death was on him if he did not fly, he lashed out with his sword killing one of the two men. The other, though wounded, still hung on grimly to the mantle. Bruce abandoned it, found his horse and rode hard after his fleeing men.

On his feet MacDougall turned to the men who had saved him. One lay dead, the other gravely hurt. In his hand he clutched the great silver reliquary brooch torn in the scuffle from the King's surtout. It was a silver circle, studded with pillared bosses surrounding a crystal dome, and the frail early morning sunshine struck shafts from it of pure gold.

At first it was as a trophy of war, won from a bloody enemy that the MacDougalls kept the ornament. But in later times, when history had made Robert Bruce the Saviour of Scotland, they held it as a sacred relic of the mighty man who had handled it and fastened it against the cold during his wandering years. And they called it reverently 'Bruce's Jewel' or 'The Brooch of Lorne'.

Three hundred and fifty years it remained a treasured possession of the clan, in times turbulent and torn with tribal strife. During that time the MacDougalls lost and won lands and keeps, honour and possessions, but no harm came to the brooch which was kept in their castle at Gylen.

Then came a day when there was conflict with their ancient enemy Clan Campbell, over a yard or two of boundary and the reiving of a few head of cattle. Gylen was taken. Campbells swarmed over it, looting its treasures and thrusting firebrands into whatever would burn. The MacDougalls seethed helplessly. But this was the way of war in old times. They could only watch flame and spark fly upwards to light the sky over what had been their sturdy castle. Then there was no brightness, only blackened walls and a pall of drifting smoke.

Some, among them Walter Scott writing later of the brooch in his story-poem 'The Lord of the Isles', said that it had been irretrievably lost in that fire with other priceless treasures. Other traditions had it that it was carried off by the Campbells as booty and kept for periods secretly by various of their clan households so that enemies did not know where to find it. Scott was mistaken but the poet's ageing, romantic heart surely warmed to a story which was passed round the coffee-houses of Edinburgh and Selkirk, seven years after his verses had recorded the loss of the brooch.

In these more civilised days of 1822 when clansmen had given up their tribal feuding and the Chief of the Campbells had perhaps taken, like almost everyone else, to reading Scott's poetry, he gave a dinner-party at which MacDougall of Lorne was his guest of honour.

Seven courses over, the ladies withdrawn, and the decanter passing hospitably round the kilted menfolk, Campbell proceeded with a small ceremony. He stood up and laid a small package before his principal visitor. Inside lay the Brooch of Lorne.

'I think, sir, that the sons of the fighting men who took this of King Robert the Bruce should hold it now and for all time coming, for it was ever truly a MacDougall spoil of war.'

Perhaps to have truly come 'home' the Brooch should now lie with the Honours of Scotland in Edinburgh, or even with the Crown Jewels at the Tower of London, but seven hundred years of safe-keeping, apart from only that period with the Campbells, surely gives moral possession to the MacDougalls. Certainly Queen Victoria did not covet it as belonging to her, when she came house-hunting at Tayside and saw it there. Another MacDougall was wearing it then as he commanded the barge which carried the Queen down Loch Tay, and Victoria wrote without envy that night in her diary, that Lorne had unclasped the pin and shown her 'the real Brooch of Lorne taken by his forefathers from King Robert the Bruce himself'.

Note: The Royal Museum of Scotland confirms that the ornament remains still, seven centuries after it was wrenched from Bruce's mantle, a treasured keepsake with the MacDougalls, at Dunollie Castle in Argyll.

BECKY LOGAN
AND THE STOLEN HEIR

In the days of perhaps two centuries ago when Becky Logan with her fair curls and rose-blush complexion was the brightest star in the company of players that strolled the west of Scotland's towns and countryside, acting was not the seemliest of ways for a lass to earn a crust. There was some little mystery among the party about what had led Becky to the boards, for she never talked about her own people. There was a reserve and something of refinement about her that suggested a douce rearing. Not the careless polish of the disowned aristocrat exactly. Something deeper than that. For Becky was not gentry. She was genteel; a condition which had required much more conscious effort on someone's part than the mere passive bequest of blue blood.

In all the time with the theatricals that she tickled the fancy of patrons or drew sighs of tragic sadness, her colleagues never heard a coarse word or saw an uncouth gesture from Becky. And they were never really close to her, for there was always that air about her that was superior to their own rough, honest earthiness.

It was therefore a matter of astonishment to them when Becky, at the age of twenty-two, ran off with a gangrel band of gipsy-tinks who were considered by the players to be a Scots mile wilder and less sober than they were themselves. As they gathered themselves together after her defection to re-distribute Becky's repertory of parts, they could only shake their heads and conclude that there must be a fair heedless streak in her somewhere to bring her, first from a good home to their company, and then off a second time with even more galravaitching folk.

The players had met up and companied with the gipsies for a week while they were on the same route through Ayrshire but had not noticed the looks and glances exchanged increasingly often between the sedate Becky and a flash-eyed Romany sporting a scarlet neckcloth and with a single gold earring glinting among his dark curls. In vain, Ma Cribben, who stitched the costumes for the plays, minded her that the ancient tink woman who read Becky's palm was the lad's fond grandmother, and warned the love-sick girl as it was moonshine to believe that in the gipsy boy she had found a destiny she must willy-nilly follow. But her wise words went unheeded.

Unlike the players, whose lodgings were at least under some kind of roof however dilapidated, Becky's new tribe slept under the stars, or at best in snell weather, under tented sackcloth. They were cunning and opportunist but they had their own code, and their own ways with those who flouted it. And when, after a week or two, Becky was wed to her Liam in a gipsy cantrip of a celebration with flowers and fiddle dancing and the ritual presentation of a pair of silver earrings matching her new man's gold ones, the same thrawn spirit that had brought her into their way of life, accepted it and grafted her without complaint equally on to its hardships and its joyful bonhomie.

Liam was as good and true, as wicked and faithless as any of the other gipsy men, and a deal handsomer. If he had a roving eye Becky turned a blind one to that and rejoiced instead in the pleasure he took in the little daughter that was born to them before a year was out.

But Becky's man was never tested as a helpmeet in old age, for when the child was just turned four, a brawl in a country ale-house, or perhaps the knife of a cuckold somewhere, made a widow of her. Liam, in paper cap and footbands, was laid unkisted on a gipsy funeral pyre, his spoon and bowl beside him and his donkey lying nearby, done to death to be his journeying companion.

Her man had always been able to coax a rare wit out of Becky and a sparkle from her eyes. The tinks had warmed to those, but now they found the giorgio-woman without them, an uneasy companion.

'Irkin' like a grain o' sand in a river oyster,' grumbled the women, jealous now of the fairness of Becky and her child. They would not have abandoned the two, but Becky was aware of their antagonism, held Tina close and drew back into her own secret soul. She bore their mutterings until the moon that had been new over Liam's funeral had come and gone, then she slipped away into the darkness one night and was five miles away from the camp by daybreak.

The old tale does not tell of all the places where Becky and her girl wandered over the next few years. They survived somehow during the round of the seasons, with a winter's kitchen service here, a harvest there, the selling of gew-gaws and gipsy-lore round farms and cottages, the reciting of ballads and the singing of songs at fairs and markets. And as the girl grew she shared the earnings of an honest penny.

When bothies or kitchen chaffs were their sleeping places they bathed at yard pumps or in steading tubs; when they lay in the leas of dykes or hedges, they rose in the mornings to the sharp tingle of cold burn water. And yet for all their hard rootless way of life, Tina grew into a comely, gentle and quiet-spoken young woman. The beauty of the countryside and the pleasure of watching its creatures in their natural haunts made her footfall light and her voice low and soft, not to disturb them. She was shy of humans other than her mother, sheltered in spite of never having had an own roof over her head.

But something else about Tina troubled Becky. Although the open air had given a lovely glow to the girl's cheeks there was a transparency about her skin that spoke a certain frailty and made her mother seek out a place in service for the girl in the late winter of her sixteenth year.

She found Tina work at last on the Bankside estate, in the laird's kitchen there, while Becky went her own free-spirited way, promising to be back when the days were warmer.

Tina was timid and winsome, graceful as a fawn and quite ignorant of the wicked ways of such fine young blades as the laird's son Ninian Buchan. When she had been some weeks at Bankside he chanced on her one day tubbing a washing at the kitchen door. He wheedled her into taking a walk with him when her chores were done. He was a handsome, merry lad to wander with, and after that first day they meandered often into the laird's woodland and kissed among the willows by the river.

In the way of his philandering world of young men with too much time on idle hands, he deceived her with sweet whispered promises. And by the time she was ready to delight his eyes with word of their coming child and claim those promises, he was off on the Grand Tour that she had never heard of, to learn about art and music in the fine theatres and galleries of Rome and Florence and Paris. Tina's education on the other hand was now complete. For word had come home that Ninian had wooed and won a lesser European contessa and would not be back until his months of honeymoon were over.

If Tina's education was finished, her unhappy young life was drawing to its close too, for, back with Becky, betrayed and prey to the winds round the barn where they had taken refuge, she died in childbirth, and her baby followed her with never even a whimper.

Stricken, Becky Logan vowed vengeance on Ninian of Bankside if it should have to wait a dozen years.

Meanwhile Ninian Buchan had come home, his wild oats sowed and ready now to cultivate tame ones on his estates. His marriage and the sudden death of his father had sobered him to settle to a life of worthy respectability and to the rearing of the child that had been conceived his heir in Florence, a bonnie lad whom they called Robin.

Nowhere near a dozen years had passed before Becky found her chance to strike at Ninian. Wherever else she had roamed in the years following Tina's death she had never remained too far from Bankside acres to watch and wait. She knew their every path and spinney and had even found her way among the gossiping women of the laird's kitchen to tell their fortunes and bring them trinkets from fairs they would never visit.

It was on one of those afternoons at Bankside that providence was kind, for a careless nursemaid left the laird's toddler son to Becky's sole care while the 'gipsy' sat in the sun at the kitchen door where Tina had first encountered Ninian himself.

By the time the nurse, having failed to find either child or gipsy visitor, was confessing her loss to the frantic parents Becky was far away along a deserted secret pathway, young Robin happed firmly in her shawl.

She had no real plan of what to do with the child or where to stay. She had no wish to harm him bodily and she could not but think that her providential stars were still in conjunction when, in a clearing among trees by the Loudon river she found a party of the Romanies she had left so long ago. She made herself known and there was no jealousy now of the ageing giorgio, bent with hardship, and rheumatic as the alders where their sacking shelters were slung. And no gipsy would have turned away a crying child.

It was Becky's third good fortune that the company was breaking camp next day and making far over the moors to the wild lands beyond Stra'ven. As she tramped with them her feet were the lighter for gloating on the revenge she had taken on Ninian Buchan.

It was many months before the laird and his sad little contessa gave up hope of ever finding their son again, or the woman who had stolen him away. At last Ninian took his lady, broken further by learning that there would never be another child, on a journey back to Florence to lift her flagging spirit and occupy her in reunion with her own family.

Perhaps if Ninian had ever known of the tragedy he had left behind when he took his first carefree Grand Tour he would earlier have become the considerate, sensitive man his own griefs made him now, for when he heard of an orphaned girl-child, presently living in the Convent of the Sacred Heart in Florence, he brought her to his Maria to be her adopted daughter.

They called her Lisa and, back home in Ayrshire, she was the delight of their eyes, the flower of their hearts, and there was no careless nursemaid this time. The girl was dark-eyed, slender and lovely and, as the years turned on, grew into a vivacious and warm-hearted young woman.

Robin, meantime, like a healthy young animal, had thrived among the Romanies. He had grown away from Becky to be simply one of the tribe, but he had taken with him the fastidious ways she had fostered in her early days as his mother-figure. He had the chestnut good looks of the Buchans, but he had also the field and river skills of his gipsy companions. He was patient to guddle idling trout and could find a rabbit for the pot or lift a straying chicken from a cot yard as quickly as any of them. And he could make magic music from an old tin-whistle as they sat round the curl of smoke from their night fire.

But as Becky grew older the surprising thought came increasingly often to her mind, that this boy on whom she doted had by rights a much greater heritage than to be a roving poacher or gipsy music-maker, and that in her old rage she had kept it from him. And when next the company trundled their donkey carts towards Bankside, for once Becky was there with them as they set camp beside the sedge-grass and buttercups at the river's edge. Next morning she drew Robin aside.

'Go you up to the laird's house, Robin-faa, and mind you look for Himself there. Tell him there's word for him from Becky the gipsy, that he'll be glad of it, and bid him here to the spinney.'

Cheerfully Robin took the path through the trees, for might there not be the chance of a fat rooster in the big-house yard? Across a stream and a field away from the mansion a dark girl in a yellow dress was gathering meadow-flowers in a corner, her back to the far fence. He savoured the picture for a moment before he saw a break in the fence and a great bull moving threateningly from his pasture towards the kneeling figure. Robin shouted, but a light wind carried his voice away from her. He pulled out his whistle and the piercing notes of a Romany frenzy startled her. She saw the bull, clambered quickly over the near fence and dashed headlong into a shallow pool in the burn between herself and Robin. He ran and gathered the dripping lass in his arms. Her fright over, she looked at him, laughed and began to struggle. But not very hard.

'Are you fae the big hoose?' he asked. His answer came when Ninian Buchan, who had watched the scene helplessly from his window, ran towards them to make sure the precious Lisa was unharmed.

'My grateful thanks to you, lad.' His hand went to his pocket for a rewarding guinea. But his horror had included, too, the sight of the kerchiefed gipsy on his land and so close to his daughter. Even as he handed over the money he detached Robin's arm from round her waist, asked with a touchy edge to his voice.

'But what mischief had y'in mind, on my acres, lad?' Robin forgot the fat rooster and simply delivered Becky's message.

'Old Beck the gipsy-wife bids you down to the spinney, for she's what she says is glad word for you.'

Ninian had good cause to mistrust gipsies, and was more concerned about the dripping Lisa than to parley with this Becky if she was one of that breed and wanted a favour of him. But even as the boy spoke, Becky came slowly along the pathway, her breath coming sore on her, partly from a failing heart and partly for the confession she had steeled herself to make.

In the early days with Robin she had never thought to restore him to his family, but as he had grown to handsome manhood she had understood the feeling her Tina might have had for his father and made up her mind to offer him back to his own people. Whatever the old woman's roots, she had long ago absorbed a glimmer of the Romany second sight and when she lifted her old eyes on Lisa, she saw long years ahead for both young people. She clasped their hands together as she haltingly laid open her sin and told Ninian for the first time, of his.

A choking rage died away in the laird as he remembered not only his dalliance with Tina but that, except for the stealing away of his son, Lisa would still have been at the Convent of the Sacred Heart.

Robin's parents would have found room at Bankside for Becky's last days.

'Best not,' she shook her head. 'Less harm done if I'm just awa' and leave ye be.'

But she was past the rigours of another winter with the gipsies and when a company of strolling players came for a season to Kilmarnock and Ninian found a place for her with them, life came full circle (for some of them were the grandchildren of her own long ago companions). She minded their bairns and stitched at the costumes as she remembered Ma Cribben doing in those old days when she had chided the young Becky for her wilful ways.

She spent a contented six-month with them before she died and was laid to rest decently in the old kirkyard near Bankside, with only the silver earrings they put beside her in the kist, as a remembrance of the years she had wandered with the Romanies.

In the 11th century when King Malcolm Canmore was not seeking to delight the pious heart of Queen Margaret with books illuminated by his monks or with the good works she loved to see him do, he had interests and pursuits of his own that he enjoyed. One of those pleasures was the hunt, and one of his favourite haunts for sport was over the lands round Kindrochit Castle on Deeside. He would leave the gentling and civilising of his court to his wife for a time and enjoy the hospitality of the Constable of Kindrochit.

The Constable had minstrels and story-tellers, jesters and gipsy-wives brought in to entertain the King during meals, and in the stretches of time between hunting forays. But another pastime, unique to Kindrochit among the Deeside keeps, was to visit a wild boar kept at the castle and watch his lumbering antics as he snouted at his food or rolled in the straw which lined the den made for him in a shallow cave near the back yard of the building. For Malcolm's pleasure the Constable would escort him there during the day and even in the light of resin flares after dark.

The King enjoyed the comic ongoings of the boar and many a time congratulated the Constable on keeping the animal so healthy and well-fed. If Malcolm had known what lay behind the beast's contentment he might have been less well-pleased with his Constable. It was perhaps a pity too that Margaret had never come to Kindrochit, for she would surely have paid kindly visits to peasant cots on the estates and heard for herself what manner of man was their host.

The Constable of Kindrochit was a bull-necked man, grisling and bristled as his pet boar, he was tough, rough-cut and harsh-spoken, and heartily hated by the plain folk of the district over whom he held sway. They were people of few worldly goods, most of them struggling for survival on overworked little patches and collectively trying to keep a small area of common grassland lush enough to graze their animals. Yet from those the Constable demanded willy-nilly the regular supply of live cattle, one at a time from every family in rotation to amuse his pet until the exhausted cow would die and then be torn apart for the boar's food.

There was grumbling among the local people who well understood the laws of feeding an animal that their families might live by its produce, and of garnering their seed-corn to invest for the next season. And so they were scandalised by the Constable's prodigal waste of their precious animals to satisfy his fat, lazy and useless pig. All the same the fear of imprisonment, or worse, contained the grumbling within their own fire-circles or among small groups simmering with anger in the open safety of the hills where they would not be overheard.

But when, in the year after her man had died, the turn came of Mistress Kate Macleod, lame and ailing herself, to sacrifice her single remaining cow, her fifteen-year-old lad, Sandy, lost all grovelling caution and decided that enough was enough. His father, Angus, had dwyned for a year or two, not able to work his ground, and all he had left as legacy was a stony strip outside his cot, the treasured cow and the doughty lad who since childhood had been able to bring down wild fowl and bird by the way he had with bow and arrow, a skill surpassing that of any other for ten miles all directions. There had been times when Angus had wished his boy as handy with spade and foot-plough. But Sandy's knack was with the bow.

When word came that the cow was now to be required of them Sandy thought first of going boldly to the Constable to plead that she should be spared. Then came the thought of the iniquity that was on the whole community and, determined to put an end to it, he made three new fine feathered arrows for his quiver and took a thoughtful tramp into the hills instead. That late, darkling afternoon he contented himself with taking a plump and lustred capercaillie that he surprised from a thicket into flight. His aim with that first arrow had been true and as he strode purposefully towards Kindrochit Castle carrying the bird, he plucked several good feathers from it for future use.

Sandy slipped quietly round the back of the castle, prepared his bow with the second of his arrows, threw the capercaillie to the front of the den and waited for the boar to come out from the dark shadows at the back. Out he rolled to turn over the bird with his snout then, holding it down with a fore-hoof, to examine it at leisure. Sandy took careful aim. His arrow sang as it flew swift and straight, and the boar pitched over, dead.

There was uproar next day around Kindrochit when the dead beast was discovered. The Constable was enraged on four counts . . . that his authority had been flouted, that the killer had escaped, that the pet was dead which so amused the King and which he had hoped would be his own passport to preferment . . . and . . . worst of all . . . that Malcolm was even now on his way to spend a night or two at the castle.

But if there was to be no boar for the King's delight there must be a villain to produce who had committed the crime. All the evidence they had were the remains of the capercaillie and the arrow that had felled the boar. The Constable had every cot and ramshackle hut searched for similar feathers to those on the killer arrow. Sandy had destroyed his own remaining arrow but forgotten the feathers he had plucked from the capercaillie.

At dawn two days later the Constable's men found them, and the boy was taken back in chains to the castle.

'So you thought, did-ye, to mock your betters and kill a royal beast? Nae man mak's a fool o' me, Sandy Macleod, and if the animal's no' here to entertain the King maybe a gibbeting'll serve instead. And just for fear you think your own cow's safe now the boar's gone, I'll see as it makes a feast to King Malcolm himself.'

And with that promise Sandy was pushed down the stone stairway and thrown into the castle dungeon.

At home Mistress Macleod wept and wrung her hands for a while. But she had more smeddum than to simply dree her weerd and leave things be.

There was but the one main track for visitors to Kindrochit and, happed in her own plaid and that of her late lamented man, she took up a place there in the shelter of a scatter of boulders and the overhang of an alder grove. There she waited on the coming of the King.

It was six hours later after that meeting with the widow, that Malcolm, knowing more of his Constable than he had over done before, reached the castle with Mistress Macleod alongside him, mounted behind one of his company. That evening sun struck long shadows from the gibbet prepared before the entrance, where young Sandy would dangle to death for the King's amusement.

The Constable began to explain as best he could why the customary snuffling of the boar would not be on the programme.

'But we've the rascal safe below there ready for his hanging,' he assured his lord. But Malcolm cut him short.

'Bring him here, Constable, for his mother tells me of his skill with the bow and I'd like fine to test it myself . . . and his mother's faith in it.'

By the time Sandy was dragged out and the chains struck off, all the cot-folk from within a mile of the castle had gathered at the gallows. The King looked long at the fair hair, ruddy cheeks and angry blue eyes. If Margaret had been at Malcolm's side the coming trial by ordeal would not have taken place, but there was still enough of the barbarian in the King to relish a good baiting.

'Bring a bow and arrow . . . and a peat for Mistress Macleod here,' he ordered. 'Now, boy, you can show me just how brave an aim you have, how steady an eye. If you shoot the peat from off your mother's head, you go free!'

The boy turned to his ashen mother, frowned and then faced his King.

'My lord, you must give me two arrows,' he said slowly.

'I am a merciful man. Take two arrows.'

Sandy's gaze met his mother's again. The peat was placed, the arrow fitted and the bow arched. Without a tremor the boy released it. The peat fell neatly apart. The trial was over.

'You have so cool a hand and eye, lad, you had scarcely need of the pair of arrows. Why did you want them both?'

The great Malcolm almost quailed before the blazing eyes that were turned on him.

'Because, my lord,' said Sandy Macleod distinctly, 'had I killed my mother wi' the first, I'd have taken you wi' the second.'

The crowd gasped and his mother all but fainted, sure now that the lad would hang for his folly. But the King knew honesty and courage when he met it.

'Your mother tells me you have more skill with your arrows than liking for the land. There's a soldier's place for you with me, if you care to bring your bow-arm there,' he offered.

'I've lost notion, some, for the bow, lord-king sir . . . but if it's a reward you're making me for your entertaining. . . . The crowd gasped again. . . . I would sooner hae a bull to sire a calf on my mother's coo!'

King Malcolm threw back his great shaggy head and laughed. He ordered the bull from the Constable's herd and moved inside to have a few grim words with his host about his heavy hand on the peasantry and to order the public roasting for them all, of the dead boar.

Sandy took his mother home that day, with such a distaste in his heart for the bow and arrow that he never lifted them again. He took to delving, tilthing, watering and generally coaxing his father's land into producing kails and grain as fair as any in the district. He grew healing and flavouring herbs, and eventually raised a small herd of worthy cows, none of which was ever fed to a boar at Kindrochit Castle.

Whatever else may be said about Mary, Queen of Scots and Henry Darnley, there is no doubt that they made a handsome couple. They may have been, as their enemies claimed, weak and wanton, vain and vicious, but they were, both of them, comely, long-limbed, graceful and fair of face. Is it not surprising then that their only son, conceived in the first glory of their infatuated love and born to them in their vigorous youth, should have been the shauchling, ugly James VI with his tendency to dribble and his unco-ordinate limbs?

It was maybe to explain this genetic puzzle that in those days of over four hundred years ago, a two-part story grew that many swore was gospel truth, while others called it spiteful legend.

There were many remarkable things about Mary Stuart apart from the learning, the ready tongue, and the magnetic charm that even her enemies acknowledged. But one that has rather slipped the notice of history was the sheer amount and variety of activities that she packed into her days. Perhaps there was some sense that there was a shortage of future in her life and she had better do as much as possible in the time that was available. Maybe that started early. After all, by the age of eighteen, had she not been Queen of Scots, betrothed to the heir of England, Dauphine, Queen and widow of France; and was now back in her own airt, come of age, to take up her Scottish throne and ready to find a suitable new husband. Eighteen.

Come from the elegance and sophistication of the French court, Mary was like a knotless silken thread in the rough fabric of Scots society. There was not even the comfort of her own Catholic background in her new capital, for its chapels, where she might have had beauty and colour on which to feast culture-shocked eyes, had been stripped to bare walls and basic furnishing during the previous two years since Scotland had been declared Protestant and the austere John Knox was at the height of his powerful popularity.

It was perhaps natural that Mary, barely out of her teens (and her widow's weeds) had turned to one or two abortive flirtations before she met and lost her wayward heart to nineteen-year-old Darnley a few years later. Various other social and political indiscretions had already dented Mary's reputation and many were sceptical of her wisdom when she set her sights on Henry Stuart.

She married him in 1565, secretly in March, or officially in July, or with the Pope's dispensation in September, which ceremony was proper depending on which found favour with which recorder. Since they met only in February, the March marriage suggests a wilfully whirlwind courtship; the public ceremony with the lavish trimmings was in July; but Catholic sticklers considered that only the Pope's dispensation for the wedding of cousins, dated September, marked the start of the true union.

Whatever the date of the marriage and of the cruelly early death of love between the partners, it is firmly documented that a son was born to them in a tiny panelled room, with a small window high above the cliff face of Edinburgh Rock.

Mary was an exhausted young woman with a quiverful of reasons for distress on what should have been a day of real happiness. There was her still-dipping moral reputation which made it seem necessary for her to swear in an anguished voice that this was the legitimate son of her husband.

'So much your son that I fear for him hereafter.' And there were other anxieties . . . the turmoil of emotions in her mind and heart, her grief at the murder of her affectionate minstrel Rizzio, the reckless growing regard for the Earl of Bothwell; and the tormenting, damning notion that all could still be well if only Darnley were dead. But among all the swirling thoughts, perhaps at this elemental moment of the gift to her from her Catholic God of a child, what distressed her most was that she would not be allowed to raise her son as a Catholic. For through all her misjudgements and foolishness her devotion to Mother Church was unswerving.

The once-upon-a-time part of the story begins from that undoubted fact.

So, troubled and anxious about these many things, Mary lay after her boy's birth soothed only by the holding of the baby in her arms. The waiting-lady who was to act wet-nurse busied herself about the child's clothing, fearful that the little prince was not the lusty child she had already at her breast and that Mary's joy in him could be as short-lived as he seemed like to be himself . . . please God not so. . . . Two other women stood quietly at the small window.

The Queen was crooning softly, then stopped suddenly with a catch of her breath.

'He must belong to the Holy Church . . . truly baptised . . . for there are those who would that he was sworn to God a Protester.'

'Lie still, my Lady. 'Tis but an hour since the Prince was born.'

Mary had had a difficult labour and delivery, and had been disturbed by Darnley's sheepish visit to see and claim his son. She was weary and, after he had gone, slept through the conspiratorial murmuring of midwife, ladies, and the few men of her own faith close enough to the Queen to be in apartments near her chamber that day. Then the voices fell silent, the attendants tiptoed about the room until Mary wakened much refreshed, and had a plan put to her concerning her son's baptism that was no wilder than those she had indulged in the past, and would surely tackle in the future.

Within a day or two, the story goes, the child was happed in extra swaddles (for although it was June there was a grey chill in the high air round the castle). A creel was discreetly whisked into the little room under a bundle of linen. Ropes were slung round it and the child laid inside and carried to the window. With anxious hearts the plotting group lifted their Prince over the sill and let him down safely to where a priest stood waiting far below to baptise the child for Rome.

Then Prince James was safely back in the chamber and Mary's heart was quietened, at least for her son's immortal soul.

A few more days and the Queen's returning health brought a fresh surge of feeling for Bothwell. Before her cleansing month was over she left Edinburgh, to be with him and escape the clouds gathering round her marriage. She danced and diced, played masques and rode with her falconers; until the realisation came that she was forgetting the features of her son's face, and must be back to Edinburgh.

After that, another jaunt, this time to the Borders where Bothwell had his keep: followed by a formal progress with her husband Darnley to Stirling, to hand over their boy to John Erskine, Earl of Mar, and his good Countess. For a brief space they were overtly a couple, two young parents, with the child in his mother's arms, taking the air, promenading the ordered gardens there where white peacocks strutted and flaunted in the early autumn sun.

The Mar family for generations past had been the traditional raisers of Scotland's royal heirs and Mary had the assurance of knowing that, among a rabble of self-seeking nobles jealously jostling for power, this Mar was an honest man who would seek the best for his charge and rear him with integrity. That the Countess had recently given birth to her own second boy would offer young James family companionship of his own age.

By now Mary's infatuation with Bothwell was more intense than her maternal instinct, for, having left James to the quiet care of the Erskines of Mar she now flagrantly pursued her affaire with him, out of sight and hearing of whatever was befalling her son.

It had already seemed to some a miracle that the child who had been exposed to so much had survived at all . . . the hatred between his parents, the knife point at his pregnant mother and his unborn self, on the night of Rizzio's murder, then the difficult birth. Now, so the tale goes, (a tangle of fact and folklore), the baby Prince and Heir of Scotland ailed with the Mars at Stirling and, despite every effort of their closest and most discreet household circles, died, in the nursery he shared with the Countess's own child. There was consternation, for it was clear that his estranged parents would never conceive another child. And so hurried conspiracy surrounded James's death as it had his birth. The tiny body was wrapped in a small silken shroud which had been lovingly embroidered with the monogram J, placed in a little kist and carried by night to Edinburgh where a recess was made for it behind the wainscoting in one of the Queen's apartments.

Back at Stirling there was loud lament that the Erskines' son had died and those outwith the inner circle grieved for the Countess and were glad that she had the care of the little Prince to occupy her mind, and his coming baptism to help arrange.

Tradition does not suggest how Mary signalled her sympathy for Lady Mar. Perhaps she sent a message or expressed it when, weeks after she had last seen James, she arrived in Stirling for the christening in December, pleased no doubt that the child was growing almost out of recognition.

As there had been more than one wedding ceremony for Mary and Darnley, tradition has it that there was more than one baptismal one for the most High and Potent Prince of Scotland. The Queen's fear, which had led to the first hidlins sacrament, that Master Knox's faction would not allow her son a Papist christening had come to nothing. In a celebration of pomp, glitter and gold plate the second son of John Erskine, Earl of Mar was baptised James Charles Stuart according to the Rites of Rome, with the absence in his own quarters of the sulking Darnley only passingly observed.

If any remarked the likeness to his surviving 'foster' brother of Mar or to other Erskines, which appears so notable in portraits, they may have put it down to the years spent in constant company with the family; of if they later criticised the grown King for doing so little for Queen Mary in her English prison years, perhaps they remembered that she had so early neglected him for Bothwell. Or, puzzled and inventive, they may have planted the seeds of a myth. . . .

Legend, lie and fiction . . . there was so much that was bizarre in those plotting, perilous six years of Mary's personal reign that nothing seems impossible. As years passed and memories grew blurred, the surviving child grew to eccentric manhood, his uncouth ways and prodigious scholarship a wonder certainly, in the Mary-Darnley offspring, but put down to the efforts of his tutors. The changeling tradition faded out of men's minds . . . almost even out of lore. Almost, but not quite. For it was remembered some three centuries later, when a fire in that part of Edinburgh Castle where these old dramas, real and imagined, were set, revealed behind gutted wainscoting, a small coffin, a silken J-marked shroud and the bones of an infant child.

Note: Mary had landed at Leith to take up her throne in the autumn of 1561 and fled finally across the Solway in the spring of 1568. In that brief space of six and a half years there had been two well-recorded murders (those of Rizzio and Darnley) and others shrewdly suspected. There were two marriages, the conception of three children, half-a-dozen stately royal progresses and as many wild flights across the country; there had been near-fatal illness, battle, suspicion, intrigue, personal religious confrontation. And almost most incredible of all, though with no bearing on the story, throughout everything, we have the picture of a skilled needlewoman patiently selecting silks and wools and plying her needle in exquisite embroidery . . . an unlikely background to the other hectic tapestry of truth and fiction that has been woven of her life. There are a dozen reasons and much scholarly evidence to make sensible people scoff at the tales of secret christening, infant substitution and wainscot casket, but that they are too far-fetched, cannot be one of them.

THE LAIRD'S CUSTOM

The Merchant Scobie of the old Edinburgh High Street had two tenement lands there, each with seven storeys to it. The mid-lands were for judges, baillies and sundry such high falutin' fine folk like himself. Indeed, did he not live in one of the best, with his dominating wife and expensive daughter? The ground floors and basements were for gangrel-folk with their goats and pigs, and for small book-keepers. The top floors were for scholars, ministers and dominies, gentlefolk without too many worldly goods, but much else to enrich their lives.

The merchant was quite under the thumb of Mistress Scobie, as much for her hearty temper and threatening posturing when he crossed her, as for the fact that her old father was principal backer of the Scobie enterprise which, without his money, would collapse. Like many a man browbeaten at home the merchant was a bully abroad, and one of the ways in which he bolstered his pride as a man, was to grant rented rooms on top and bottom floors, only in return for favours. These might be simple things from basement tenants, like the regular provision of milk by one of the herds or of fire logs from a labouring man . . . or from the book-learned in the attics, free clerical work, accounting, or even an hour's story-reading to the merchant's supper guests. And there was one other, which remained a secret between him and the individual who rendered it.

One of the tales that had been read to a Scobie gathering at one time concerned the medieval custom that a laird might claim the wedding-eve of a bonnie bride-to-be among his tenants. Others present had enjoyed the story and dismissed the ritual as a barbarity of past times, but Archibald Scobie had thought it no bad thing, and quietly put it into practice himself, initiating a number of wenches, among those to whom he gave lodging, into the married state, before their bridegrooms had the chance. He chose carefully, of course, only the shy lasses in from country places, away from their families and too frightened of Scobie and of not having a married roof over their heads . . . too innocent too, to tell their lads lest they abandon them for shame. The time he chose for his advances was when the young men were off elsewhere in the town, working and out of the way for an hour or two.

Young Alison Ker was surely just such a girl. A Border lass with no father or brothers on hand to be watching over her, she was his wife's personal maid and seamstress, bonnie, near to beautiful. Anytime he chanced on her in his wife's company he had seen her docile and quietly at work. There would be no trouble from her. She was soon to be wed to young Peter Adair, presently dominie out Penicuik way, but after his marriage, to be teacher in an Edinburgh schoolroom. It suited the merchant fine that the bridegroom would arrive in the town only on his wedding morning. Scobie had given them an employer's blessing and, at a time of crowded tenements and homeless couples, had generously found an attic landing for them. It was a good square room with a narrow back stair into the courtyard as well as the common one up from the street entry.

The merchant's wife might have been a scold and martinet with her man, but she had ever been a fair mistress to Alison Ker and, save for giving her a small bundle of linen to take with her to mend, she had allowed the girl away early, this day before her wedding, to go to her new attic-lodging a hundred yards up the High Street, and prepare it ready as her married home.

'Never heed to bring back the sewing tonight, Alison lass, for I've a mind to see your place when your bits and pieces are placed and your bed set out wi' that bonnie cover. Maisie'll light me up the street and carry it back wi' me.'

So Alison hummed happily as she spent the afternoon scrubbing and cleaning, opening the window-chink shutters to the fresh air and rubbing up six platters from Selkirk and four drinking cogs Peter had brought from his mother. She noticed that the door snib was broken, but he would fix that when they settled in. She put her dishes on the shelf, spread up the bed, sprinkling sweet herbs between the covers and thought she might even sit up all night in the chair, not to spoil the bed for her wedding night. She set Peter's books, his papers and an ink-horn ready for him on a side table. From the basket she brought out a small cask, a whisky-boss that she set on the centre table beside a water-jug. She laughed softly, putting her chestnut head to one side as she considered it. It had been a gift from her Selkirk blacksmith father . . . a raw fiery brew from his private still, hidden in the nearby moors.

'Peter'll no drink that Faither. It tak's great farmin' men to stomach your field usque.'

'You tak' it, lass. It'll staun' you good, gin there's illness, wi' hot water and a spoon o' honey.' Privately he thought it a great waste to use whisky that way, but the herb-wives down Selkirk way, swore by it for a cure of most ailments. It would do no harm for the lass to have it for ill-chance.

The little home ready for the dominie coming next day, inviting as she could make it, Alison sat down with Mistress Scobie's sewing, which was but pillow-covers wanting a stitch and was soon done. She laid it aside and went to close the shutters against the night air. The passing show on the High Street always fascinated her. At this hour there were herds with their animals, pedlar billies, a pair of clergymen from the High Kirk . . . there were women late home with their washing, and laughing maidservants slopping well-water from their buckets over their clogs. Amongst the throng she glimpsed Merchant Scobie, stout and florid, strutting pompously up the cobbles in his braws, his fancy blue coat and breeches, his white hose and buckled shoon . . . going no doubt on a business call.

Presently he was out of sight, too close to the side of the street to be in view any longer. She turned back to the room, admired it again and re-arranged the plates on the shelf.

When she heard the sound of footfall on the main stair and its stopping outside her own entry, she supposed Mistress Scobie had come two hours earlier to pay her visit and went to open up. But the unlocked door was already open and it was the merchant himself stood there, come surely at his wife's bidding for the sewing. He stepped inside and looked round.

'You've the place right trig, lassie. Mind, it's a good land I've let you have and they're no' easy come-by.'

'We're obliged t'you, Merchant Scobie sir, and you'll get your rent reg'lar.'

'I'm sure, I'm sure . . . but mind, there's a bit more due to me than just the rent, I think.' He chucked her playfully under the chin and she stepped back. He had put a hand on her waist a time or two before, but that had been simply when his wife's back was turned in the same room and she'd taken it only as a jest. Now she was alone with him up in this crow's nest and she didn't fancy at all the look in his eye.

'Come noo, lassie. It's an auld custom to gie your laird your weddin' eve, y'ken that.' He took off his hat, spun it on to the bed, and ran a pudgy hand across her shoulder. He was strong for all he was paunchy, and Alison knew it would have to be her wits and not her brawn that would save her.

She let his hand slip down her arm and then jouked away. She tossed her head.

'I'm no one of your Grassmarket wenches, Merchant Scobie, so we'll no go at it rough. Sit you doon here first and tak' a taste o' my faither's acky-vity, to wish Peter and me good in our marriage.'

She took down two stoups, went to the table and poured him up a generous serving and, her back turned to him, took water in her own. Her teeth grated as he sat in Peter's chair and drank, screwing up his face as the Selkirk 'stilling seared his throat and went down like a rush of flame, warming him to the toes of his fine shoon. She drank from her own. He watched her.

'You're a wild lass as can tipple spirit like that, Ailie Ker.'

'It's Border stuff Master Scobie, we're bred to it Selkirk way. Will you tak' some-more, the leavin's doesnae rest well in the cask.'

Twice more she topped him up. The rage of it went through him and he felt his limbs slacken pleasantly, making the next prospect seem the more delicious. He reached out for her and slumped off the chair. She helped him to the wall-bed and loosened his neckcloth.

'Guid sakes, Merchant Scobie sir, there's a tear here in your coat and a button off your breeches. Gie me them off and I'll stitch them up for you, afore you go.' And she began to strip the top clothes off him as he lay.

He chuckled sleepily. My, but she was a wench wi' more comehither spirit than he'd thought, to be playing with him like this. For she'd aye looked douce and prim, bending over his wife's broidery or laying out her dresses. He turned on his side to grasp her, but she was floating away from him. Well, no matter, a doze first would tantalise them both the better.

Alison lit a tallow and, while he slept, sat sewing quietly, tugging each stitch firmly, one ear cocked to the bed, the other to the main stair outside. In spite of the placid picture she made there of the little seamstress sitting in the soft light, inside she was tingling, not with titillation, but to get the timing right on the next chapter of the night's adventure. Once or twice she went anxiously to the window and opened the shutter and from there, at last, she saw Mistress Scobie led by a little kitchen maid with her lantern, making her way towards the street entry just as the bellman cried the hour she had promised for her visit.

Alison shook the fuddled merchant awake.

'Master Scobie sir. The mistress is comin' . . . comin' here up the stair. She mustna find you here!' Mention of his robust wife's name startled Scobie near sober and he rolled with an oath out of the bed, groping for his clothes.

'Go you doon the back stair and put them on as you go.' She threw him the coat and breeches, planted his fine hat on his head and bundled him out to the open narrow back stair.

She watched him for a few moments struggling with the clothes, trying to get himself into the breeches and coat she had stitched tight round the legs and cuffs. The last she saw of him that night (or any other, except from a safe distance across his wife's apartments, for she had bested him once and could do it again) was of a wild figure dancing across the back court-yard in his undergarments, his outer ones flying like banners around him; his face red as a bubbly-jock's, in the light of lamps carried to and fro across the yard by people going to their evening entertainments.

Alison laughed softly, smoothed up the bed, greeted Mistress Scobie, glowed with her praises and with the little maid-servant's sighs of envy.

Later she tidied round again and lifted the usque cask to the shelf. It was nearly empty. But she would get more from her father, for it was maybe as good a safeguard as a new door lock.

THE TREASURE
OF GOLDBERRY HEAD

Tom Twomay was a better judge of a sound little ship and the ways of the wind to sail her, than he was of the men to voyage with him.

His old grandfather who had left him the *Irish Molly*, had done his little bit of trading hugging the coast from Carnlough, by Cushendun and Rathlin Sound to Londonderry. But Tom was young and more adventurous and was set to seek his fortune in wider waters.

He sat in the harbour inn one evening.

'Sure I'll cross the North Channel and up the Clyde Frith . . . Ayrshire way, for there's fair winds and good trade there w' the whole of Scotland's wealth behind it. There's glass and sugar, fine wool and leathers, and merchants to buy our goods from Ireland.'

Pet Quick, in his wild yellow pullover, put down his ale-jar and listened.

'I'll tak' a berth w' you, Tom Twomay,' he said, his small eyes glittering at the thought of easy fortune. Fat O'Shaunessy, in the great thigh-boots he'd looted from a wreck, edged along the bench.

' 'Tis a sea-road I know well, Tom lad. And whiles we could loop round Managhan and fetch up some of the French wines and perfumes that's still "contra" there. Now there's fortune for you!'

Tom Twomay had no notion to find his pot of gold in the Isle of Man smuggling, for was it not a dirty and violent game nowadays? But he could do with men to sail with him. Pet Quick was a Carnlough lad of fishing and small ships, like himself . . . strong and young. He would do well enough, sure he would. And O'Shaunessy had assured him that he knew the seven seas like his own backyard. He was lumbering and heavy, but Tom was awed by his experience.

The Old Man that was his Granda's friend, smoked his clay pipe and sat watching as Tom caulked and painted and set up his ship down by the jetty. The Old Man was quiet except that between silences he had a word of advice for Tom about oil and varnish, best gear and sailcloth. He had shaken his head over Pet Quick and O'Shaunessy.

'Greedy de'ils the both. Take care.' Tom laughed.

'If it's a fortune you're for, Old Man, 'tis greedy men y'need.'

'You're no' a greedy lad yersel' Tom-boy, but just mibbe for adventure.' That was true. The fortune was a romantic thought, but he was a contented lad and a decent competence would do him fine.

'I'll share my fortune wi' you, Old Man,' he promised, only half-jesting, for his Granda's friend was poor and there was many a day he ate nothing more than a bowl of broth a neighbour handed in.

Pet Quick and O'Shaunessy were good enough companions, Pet was willing and nimble, with muscles and brawn that were fuelled by thoughts of rich pickings up Scotland way. O'Shaunessy had told the truth, or something near it, about knowing the sea-lanes of the world and, while he was not a glutton for hard work, (aside from the rubbing and polishing of his dandy boots) he was an old hand on a ship and could keep Tom right when there was question. He had a fund of yarns too, about every mortal coast place that was mentioned. Going up the Frith they had the tale off him, of the jewels of the Spanish Armada ship that had gone down ten fathoms.

'Still lies on the sea-bed maybe, just back there off of Portencross. And there's the great Norwegian brooch somewheres, that they say King Haco lost after the Largs battle near six hundrit year ago.'

The man had a bawdy humour too, that kept them going when the weather was bad.

And for the first two or three voyages the weather surely was bad, the Carrick coast ghosted with sea-mist and the Frith dank and grey and sunless.

The two men grumbled from time to time that there was no fortune showing yet . . . no great profits, and that Twomay had cut them short a time or two when they were setting up doubtful private deals of their own. He had hasted them back to the *Irish Molly* before they had the law on them. They smouldered about the smuggled Frenchy brandy they had thought to load in Tom's hold along with the honest goods, and about a sackful of goods O'Shaunessy had lifted from under the nose of a decent merchant, that Twomay had made them leave behind. There was no fortune yet, to be sure, but Tom was content to study the ways of wind and sea, and learn his merchanting trade. He would find the fortune by and by.

For their fourth voyage the weather had changed, the shrouds had lifted from the shorelands and hills of Scotland; the sun shone and light winds filled *Irish Molly's* sails scudding them along. For the first time since they had gone adventuring together Scotland could be seen smiling in the late afternoon sun, and glowing red golden as it began to sink.

Tom Twomay ran a tight routine of rest and watch and, in this fair and steady weather, two could rest or sleep and the third take the wheel. It was Pet Quick's watch now. O'Shaunessy curled his bulk into a coil of rope and slept noisily as ever and Tom, watching the last fling of the sun's rays and going over in his mind the despatch of cargo and the handclasp bargains he would make next day, soon drowsed off, trusting the *Molly* to Pet's care.

When he woke it was not with the usual easing of limbs and the slow raising of eye-lids to light. He was sharp and alert, roused by a sudden sense that the ship was drifting. They were past the dark red mass of Ardneil cliff on Portencross Headland, with its huge triple top-slabs they had heard called The Three Nuns. To the port side not so far away had been the sheltering hills of Arran and Kintyre beyond. The evening was calm, the sun had dipped out of sight now but he should have been able to see the outline of the man at the wheel and his wild yellow jersey. There was neither sight nor sound of Pet anywhere about the ship. He roused O'Shaunessy and together they strained their eyes across the water to each side and far back in the ship's wake. There was nothing to be seen. There had been no storm. Pet was alert, familiar with the *Molly* and he had been in good enough spirits other than his impatience for profit. Had he gone down after a drinking of the spirits Tom Twomay had forbidden on board? There had been sulking when Tom had said there would be no room yet again for illicit goods on the return journey. Had Pet Quick slipped overboard to swim ashore and pursue some trade of his own or find an easier boat-master? There was nothing to be done and *Irish Molly* went on her way with Twomay and O'Shaunessy. As they would do later back in Ireland they reported the loss ashore here.

When they did, only one ancient sailor quizzed Tom closely as to precisely where and when they had missed Pet Quick, . . . then wagged his beard, 'ah-ha'd' and turned away.

When, on their return, they passed The Three Nuns of Ardneil again, it was early and the morning mists were not yet cleared away. They gazed over the veiled sea as if they half-expected to see some sign of Pet, but there was nothing, and soon they were past Ayr and out into the North Channel.

After two days at home, they stowed the hold again with deliveries for Largs, and Tom had orders in his pocket to bring back meal and meat from Irvine and a small pig for Malacky Graham at Ballymena.

The afternoon with the same bright sinking of the day was twin to the one when they had lost Quick (a freak sunset they had called it up the coast). The last of the sun streamed across from Kintyre as they sailed up the Frith. Twomay had done his stint at the wheel and O'Shaunessy was there now. As Tom had been doing the week before, he was sitting dovering, half-asleep, facing Arran and the sun. And just as on that other day he woke, a little way past Ardneil and the The Three Nuns of Portencross, instantly alert and aware that the *Irish Molly* was going her own sweet way, not into danger but like a free spirit, jaunting the waves. There was no sign of O'Shaunessy, neither bulk nor grand boots. The wheel swung gently with no hand on it. Just as before, the sun had gone down beyond Cumbrae and the tip of Arran, and, in disbelief and panic Tom's eyes raked the waters around him. All his days, back in Carnlough he had laughed at the old wives' tales and at the sea-leprechauns and he wondered now if this was a judgement on him. He sat down for a moment, head in hands, to say a prayer for the soul of O'Shaunessy, or was it for his body? Then he took the wheel, trembling at the thought of telling again the self-same story when he went ashore, of men disappeared without reason.

It was strange to Twomay, the queer way they asked about the weather, the time and the place O'Shaunessy had been lost, then when he answered, slid flat eyes away from his face to each other, and never thought to ask if he had done away with his crewmen himself.

Next day Tom took his little cargo and set off for home, his only company this time the special pig for Malacky Graham. He hadn't been overly fond of his fellow fortune-seekers but they had been his sea-mates and he knew he would feel a blackness on him when he reached The Three Nuns rocks. Yet again a third time the sun streamed towards Ardneil headland from the west, bronzing the sea. But this time Tom Twomay was not drowsing.

The three slabs of rock looked for all the world like tombstones, and he shivered at the fey thought that they were for Pet Quick,

O'Shaunessy and . . . merciful God . . . maybe for himself!

Then all at once the little ship was level with the red stone cliff. Tom stared at the high, wide rise of it above the sea, mesmerised by this new sun-drenched view. For, studding the face were great gleaming gold berry-shaped bosses and, around them like myriad twinkling stars, surely were diamonds, striking shafts of brilliance in all directions . . . a massive cliff encrusted with jewels. Then he remembered, suddenly clear, O'Shaunessy's story of the Spanish Armada, a treasure and the brooch of Haco; and he wondered if it had been lifted in some wild storm and flung against the cliff to lodge there, unseen except in the sunsets that they had said in Irvine came for a few evenings together no oftener than every seven years. He understood then about Quick and O'Shaunessy, and was nearly overcome himself to swim ashore and climb to scratch out his fortune from the cliff. But the pig squealed and he remembered Malacky and the others waiting for the meal and mutton. And, honest merchant that he was, kept his hand to the ship and sailed his cargo for Carnlough. But he would be back. Sure, one diamond just, one gold berry of that vast treasure, would be wealth for life.

He told no one there, but the Old Man.

'I'll find my jewel, Old Man, and share my fortune wi' you.' And he turned back his ship that very day.

The *Irish Molly* took no promised cargo this time, and no orders. This was a hunt for Eldorado and must not be kept back for pigs or pokes.

He slid into the channel in front of the gold berry cliff. The sunset weather had held, striking shafts again from diamond and gem. Tom made calculations with his ship's instruments to gauge the easiest reaches towards them from what looked like footholds. He steered the ship to some boatman's slipway nearby, anchored, waded to the shore. Then he leapt lightly on to a crescent of sand and, looking up towards the magic crevices, shook the wetness off himself like a great Irish collie dog.

Twice he tried the sheer climb towards his target, but there were no rock juts, and any dents were too shallow for footholds. He came down to check his route again.

He had hoped to be alone in his seeking, but the second time he dropped on to the shore, there was a girl there, slim, barefoot, shawled, and gathering cockles in a creel. He picked up two-three and dropped them into her basket.

'You dinnae want them yoursel'?' she asked in a voice, sweet as music.

'No, sure it's other pickings I'm after.'

'You're after the rock diamonds,' she said, calm as you please.

'I am so. It is diamonds is it? And the great brooch o' Haco.'

'You'll no get the Norseman's jewel, for it's found years since and's in safe keepin'. But aye, they do say it's diamonds, big as nuts and gold flashing knobs of precious stuffs an' all. They're to be seen only when we has a day or two of these unchancy sunsets. But it's a greedy man would try to tease them out. There's many a one been lost in the trying. They found a dead sailor in a yellow genzie, not two weeks since, fallen from the face, and after him, just a day or two ago, a drowned man in great fine boots full of the sea, tryin' to come ashore fae some ship, after the diamonds. Buried them in the old kirkyard, the both.' Tom would pay his respects later to Pat Quick and O'Shaunessy.

'Has the folk hereabouts no use theirselves of the treasure, to go hunting it?' asked Tom.

'None here has ever tried that I can mind, for they say the three Wise Nuns guards them, against the day when Scotland needs them for poverty's sake. But that's maybe because they think its death-dangerous to climb the face.'

Tom looked up a time or two more . . . but, as the girl talked in that lilting voice, he lost the taste for risking death just to fill the *Molly's* hold with gems from the cliff, for her hair was like spun gold, her eyes sparkled brighter than the diamonds, and there was something in her more desirable than either.

He was a bonnie lad himself with the Irish eyes of him and the sea-ruddy cheeks. She looked at him and liked what she saw.

'Aye, there's jewels there, right enough, but you're wet to the skin and cold. Come you to my father's cot, share our fire and sup . . . and think no more on treasure.'

She took him by the hand and led him past grey lichened rocks, through a coppice under the cliff, of ash and hazel; and he never looked back once to the treasure the Wise Nuns were guarding.

There was much trade for a trusty craft like *Irish Molly*, far up the Clyde Frith and among the islands, and it was two years and a day before Tom Twomay delivered and bought in Carnlough again. In the village street he met the Old Man, his granda's friend, frailer but still with memory intact.

'It's never Thomas Twomay after this long time.' And he put a scrawny hand on Tom's arm. 'You've been seeking your fortune far away.'

'Sure 'tis me, Old Man.'

'Tell me, boy-o, did you find that treasure your heart was set on?'

'Aye, so, Old Man. I did. I found my jewel, but it's, after all, no' one t'I can share wi' you,' answered Tom (though he gave his friend every groat that was in his pocket that day). And he told the Old Man of the small cot under the Gold Berry cliff, where he lived with the golden-haired, sparkle-eyed girl for wife, their bairn and the good-father who looked to his little family when Tom Twomay sailed the *Irish Molly* round the Scottish isles, trading for more modest fortune.

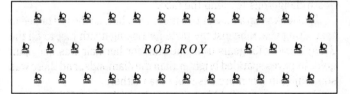

ROB ROY

If Rob Roy Macgregor's birth had been in any other century he might have lived and died a peaceable cattle-dealer and highland gentleman, with no worse than a small taste for the sporting 'lifting' of a few head of the cattle that passed through his lands. But he was born in 1671 and ahead lay turbulent and divisive times for the monarchy in Britain. All the same, that was still in the future, and in Glen Gyle at the head of Loch Katrine where the Macgregor

home was, his green years were quiet and purposeful, and his sur-
roundings a constant source of interest to the boy. He roamed its
every path, woodland, brae and burnside and there, too, he prac-
tised skills with broadsword, dagger and pistol . . . for his own
delight, for he had no real forseeable use for them. Nevertheless
they were to torment authority to fury in later years.

Glen Gyle lay between the wild highland cattle-lands to the
north and the rich farming stretches to the south, and was criss-
crossed by the tracks along which drovers brought their cattle,
making for the tryst-markets at Crieff, or to the lush grazing fields
of the south. Those between-lands were exposed and silent,
plagued by plundering reivers who could round up half a droving
with a band of seven or eight men . . . more ruthless men than
the young Rob Roy seemed ever likely to be.

He and his family farmed some of their land but there was a
better living to be had from the cattle . . . not only the raising of
their own herds but in three other ways relating to the general
trade. Rob, intimate with every yard of his native country, its
screes and hills, burns and gullies, and skilled himself at the droving, was by the age of twenty the family's principal cattle man. He
bought and sold at the trysts and offered himself for a good fee to
wealthy landowners as 'protector' of their herds as they passed
through the surrounding country. And where a landowner was not
willing to pay for such help, Rob was not above helping himself to a
head or two of cattle, to show just how necessary was the protection that he sold.

It was all no better, and no worse, than any other local man of
spirit would have done with even half of Rob's own fleetness over
known terrain and his threatening expertise with weapon and
targe.

So that was Rob Roy in his twenties; dealer, 'protector' and
occasional reiver and, alongside these cattle-trade activities,
wooer and winner of his kinswoman Helen-Mary Macgregor.

The couple settled to married life, first in a cottage at Portnel-
lan, not far from his home soil in Glen Gyle. Then since his activities had begun to show him a force in the clan the Chief made him a
more suitable award of land at Inversnaid on Loch Lomondside to
build a family home there.

As his children began to arrive, Rob looked like being as solid a member as any other of that part-wild part-tame community. But times were changing. As Queen Anne aged, hopes began to stir of restoring her brother James to the throne; and Jacobite days had arrived. Rob Roy had some sympathy for that cause but was still pre-occupied with his cattle interests. The Duke of Montrose of the time favoured the opposite side, that of the government the present monarch and her chosen Hanoverian successor. Nevertheless Rob's shrewd knowledge of the cattle trade stood him head and shoulders above any other dealer and so the two made a business arrangement, in which Montrose handed over a thousand pounds to Macgregor for the purchase of cattle at the next market, with the land at Inversnaid as security. Rob entrusted his chief drover, MacDonald Mhor, with the money, but he was a better judge of a beast than of a steward. The temptation was too much for MacDonald and he absconded with the thousand pounds.

Without waiting to report the loss to Montrose, Rob Roy set off in furious pursuit, ranging over every likely escape path and hiding-place so that, as whispers of the matter filtered back to the Duke, it seemed as if Rob was a fugitive-partner in the crime.

All Montrose's distaste for the Jacobite in Macgregor rose up, alongside his fury over the theft. He planned a mean and far-reaching revenge which would assuage his anger, help the Government cause, and at the same time bring down a man he hated . . . the Campbell of Argyll. Rob Macgregor would be his tool to disgrace this man, who had for long vied with him for power in the west, and whose family had been enemies of his own for generations.

Rob Roy was certainly a small-time rustler, but he was not a great embezzler on the thousand pound scale, and he came back honestly enough to negotiate amends with Montrose.

'I'll deal wi' you, Macgregor and make you mercy if you'll speak against Campbell Argyll and name him a conspiring Jacobin.' But Rob Roy was no more false witness than major criminal.

'That I canna do, my lord Duke. I'll never put on any man a loyalty he doesna stand up and swear for himself. Let Argyll declare his ain leanin's and no' be named by me.'

All Montrose's storming and threatening would not move his debtor and, before Rob had made back to his wife and children at Inversnaid, Montrose had despatched his factor to seize the Macgregors' stock and stores and to evict from their house Helen-Mary and her family, into the open cold of the midwinter darkness without prospect of any other refuge.

That bitter day and night in 1712 turned Rob Roy Macgregor from a land-holder, family man, small-time entrepreneur and petty reiver, into notorious, freebooting pirate and declared outlaw. And so the wild legend of Rob Roy began.

With Helen-Mary and the family settled in comparative safety in a house in Glen Dochart, offered to them by the grateful Campbells of Argyll, Roy began a life of avenging plunder. His victims were the better-off Montrose tenants, and his satisfaction was to re-distribute some of their wealth to the poorer crofters trying to scratch a living from their small strips of land.

With a select band of kinsmen he would swoop silently down on the well-provided, lifting grain and cattle from their homes in surprise attacks at pistol and dagger point . . . and, if it was possible, to gain entry to counting rooms near term days, to relieve furious householders of the money they had ready to hand over to Montrose in rent. For the struggling poor, who found themselves in arrears, he had other arrangements. He would call on the cot of some old body, or of a widower man at his wit's end for his rent, and leave enough cash to cover their back dues . . . and mind them to be sure to have a receipt from the factor when he came collecting. Then, at some strategic spot, the Rob Roy band would wait patiently for the rent man, ambush him and take back the money, leaving him short of Montrose's rent, but the receipt safely in the hands of the grateful householder.

As success followed success in small incidents Rob grew bolder. He became the scourge of the Montrose countryside, cocking a snook at the Duke at every opportunity. Neither man nor beast moved in the hills or glens without Rob's spies reporting to him destinations and routes of rent-men and herds. Factors effecting evictions of small crofters were challenged and turned away. Confiscated goods were taken back at pistol point and restored to owners and, sometimes, to compound these felonies, agents themselves were taken ransomed back to the outraged Montrose.

The Jacobite cause was gaining support and Rob found another way to torment the Duke and his fellow Hanoverians by making taunting displays of defiance. Once the Macgregors swept into Crieff, surrounded the mercat cross and raised a loud toast to the exiled 'King'. This was more a show of boldness than from real dedication to James, and if it produced a few recruits to the Cause it was but a by-product of a noisy exploit.

From time to time too, caches of government arms were raided when Macgregor weapons ran low, and now tales of his ventures against the Hanoverian Montrose began to turn Rob, in official minds, from mere sympathiser to committed Jacobite plotter. He became a fugitive from not only the Duke but from government agents, and there began then a concerted effort to capture and punish him.

But soldiers of a government two hundred miles away, and household troops of a Duke more at home in his castle than in the hills, were no match for one who had grown up as a creature of his own territory. Time and again Rob escaped them and lived to tell his grandbairns of the most savoury of such episodes. There was the time when taken, mounted and hand-tied behind a guard and progressing along a path by the River Forth, he managed to slip the strap from his wrists, drop from the horse and plunge into the swirling waters. He abandoned his plaid to draw his captors' fire and swam off to safety in the dark. Some time later, newly taken as prisoner to Logierait Castle, he fuddled his guards with a dram or two from his flask, so that they carelessly handed over their keys and allowed him walk to freedom. But the memory that the outlaw cherished more than any other of those times, when he scarcely knew what it was to sleep in his own bed, was from a night when he took refuge in the deep recesses of a cave above Loch Katrine. It happened that the party searching for him decided to give up the chase that night, and settled themselves in the front area of the same cave, where they lit a fire and happed themselves ready for sleep. At his chosen moment, with pistol cocked and dirk unsheathed, Rob stepped out into the flickering of their firelight and terrified them into flight.

After half a dozen further abortive attempts on the outlaw the embarrassed authorities seemed ready to acknowledge that they were wasting their time and energy trying to take and keep so slippery a quarry, who was by now heartily supported and succoured wherever he went, by silently cheering local people.

Rob was now nearly fifty years old and, although neither wearied nor browbeaten, was ready, for his part, to take up the more open life of the cattle trade again and settle back to family life in a new house at Balquidder. He mellowed a little, although characteristically ready to adventure out occasionally on forays he thought just . . . or perhaps lucrative. He was still the finest, canniest drover in the Trossachs and was well-employed trysting cattle for landowners (though Montrose never trusted him again). But in time he did hand over the more doubtful 'protection' business to a kinsman and moved into his evening years enjoying the prosperity he had brought lately to Balquidder, the more constant companionship of Helen-Mary and the memory of wilder days.

Perhaps he wondered in his final weeks of illness how it could be that, after such a stormy life, he was to die peacefully in his own bed. Not to go too meekly when the moment came, he had himself propped up and dressed, dirk and pistol at his side and broadsword on the wall. Then he made his farewells and bade his piper to play him out, to an ancient lament.

Note: There are well researched and chronicled biographies of Rob Roy Macgregor, following his career in the kind of detail not carried by a book of simple stories. But some small account of a man, whose name is as familiar to Scots as Robin Hood's to the English, cannot properly be left out entirely of a collection of Scottish tales.

Once upon a time there lived among the Cairngorm Mountains a farmer called Duncan MacIntosh. Like all the MacIntoshes, of his own and two generations past, Duncan was a fine handsome figure of a man who looked out over the heads of most of his fellows from a pair of blue eyes, clear as Loch Morlich on a brave, bright day. He was an honest, kindly man too and his acres turned him quite a bonnie penny.

So it was a matter of some wonder locally that his wife Betsy was such an unprepossessing woman . . . nay, not just unprepossessing but positively plain. And to compound the picture, the couple had seven daughters, not one of them with the comeliness of their father, but growing up one after the other, unbonnie like their mother. Mistress Betsy should have been in her prime for she had wed young in the days when she had been pert and attractive if not lovely, and she was now barely forty. She kept a trig, thrifty house, was even-tempered and had reared her girls douce and clever-handed. Perhaps it was the effort of raising her family, running her home, taking her share of the farm work and seeing to a difficult elderly father, who lived nearby, that, over the years, had made Betsy grow dowdy and careless of her own appearance, and dulled her bright nature. And as she had let herself go, as she had forgotten to brush her hair and trim her waists with ribbon or braid, she did not notice either that her lasses never wore a pretty kerchief, or had a bright buckle to their Sabbath shoes. Nor did she see that they had noticeably less sparkle than girls from other crofts or in the village.

All the same, Betsy had always thought that she and her Duncan were well-contented together as man and wife, and she looked forward to another half life-time jogging comfortably along with him as they had always done.

But then, around the time that Betsy was about to turn forty, she had the first uneasy suspicion that her man was straying, and had a fancy-lady somewhere. Two or three times of late he had ridden off towards Inverness for no seeming reason, and making no explanation when he came back.

Then there were the quick, furtive glances she noticed him casting over her, as if afraid she might be suspecting him. When, at last, she caught the drifting scent of lavender off his clothes after the third visit to town, she was sure.

Now, a wise, intimate friend might have advised Betsy to fight her rival by prettying herself up a bit and setting herself to re-charm Duncan, but she had long-since lost touch with the companions of her youth who might have tried to put her right. And even if she had had such friends she would never have confessed her torturing suspicions to any of them. She looked sorrowfully at her daughters, wondering if their father was going to bring shame on them too.

When yet another day came, on which Betsy realised that her man was not to be seen in his field or about the yard, and one of the girls said she had seen her father saddle up his mare earlier and ride off towards Aviemore, the poor woman, without thinking where exactly she would look for him and his sinning partner, set off on foot after him.

But she had not gone more than half-a-mile past the Alvie loch on the path along by the trees when she saw him. Far ahead in the shelter of a scatter of rocks, his mare cropping quietly alongside at the short grass, her own man Duncan MacIntosh stood in broad daylight with a figure in green in his arms, a beauty for sure, slim and swaying slightly there before him. He held her out at arms-length for a moment as if to look at her, and then he gathered her close again burying his face against the wicked bonnie green of her.

Heedless with angry grief, and determined now only to confront the pair, Betsy scrambled towards them, scratching herself on thicket and bramble and bruising her feet on yirdfast stones on the moorland. At last she was there and threw herself on them, blinded by her tears and ready to beat her fists furiously against them.

But instead, she found herself alone with Duncan, held tenderly in his arms while he stroked back her hair and wiped away her tears. The 'woman', no more she saw now than a silky green dress, lay in soft folds where he had dropped her on the ground.

'I thought it was a beautiful woman,' whispered Betsy.

'Na, na', said Duncan. 'It's *for* a beautiful woman, that's near forgotten she's beautiful . . . that's been tired and sad. Och, it's maybe been my blame, but I thocht to find a cloth length in Inverness to match the green of her eyes and get Mistress Macdonald at Aviemore to make a fine dress of it, to make her shine again.'

And now Betsy understood the lavender too, for Mistress Macdonald at Aviemore was a grand mixer of sweet herbs to make scented sachets and pot-pourris. She kissed him and then picked up the dress. Immediately she felt a warm glow sweep over her at the touch of the silk that had been bought in love. All the tension of jealousy and misery fell away. She held it against herself, smiling. Duncan admired it and saw with pleasure the rise of colour in her pale cheeks, and the sparkle that was in the green eyes.

'Every mile or so I was holding it up to see you in it, and wonder if it was right for size too.'

Betsy carrying the gown and Duncan, with one arm round her and the other leading the patient mare, they walked home, as much in love again as they had been twenty years before.

As they entered their own yard, the sash of the dress caught on a spray of bramble and a tiny scrap was torn off. One of the seven plain daughters pounced on it fondling it as part of the first pretty thing she had seen in her home for many a day. And now her eyes shone, she smiled and her quiet unanimated face became suddenly lovely. Then the mother knew that the love that had been in the buying of the dress had touched her daughter too. The broad sash was small sacrifice to make from the rest of the gown and soon all the girls had pieces of green silk to stitch into handkerchiefs, and became beautiful.

In time, as they grew into good and winsome women, and married upstanding men, the girls had daughters of their own and grand-daughters. The small kerchiefs and eventually others made from the worn dress, were passed on down the family and it became a byword from Newtonmore to Carrbridge that the generations of Duncan MacIntosh and his much-loved wife were invariably characters of beauty, wit, charm and goodness.

As for Betsy and Duncan themselves, well . . . they, of course, lived happily ever after.

SAINT AND SALTIRE

Whatever they may have called a collection of Saints in days gone by, pride, swarm, covey or herd, there was a wheen of them with Scottish connections however vague, that formed a holy mesh to support the faithful. There were Colm, Mirren, Ninian, Magnus, Cuthbert, and as many others as there are now kirks or chapels in their names.

In the oldest of all Christian days (in whatever Scotland was then called) Saint Peter himself was Father-Saint and remained so until his brother Andrew took that place. And so, while there's a rare affection most places for Saint Columba and many make pilgrimage to Iona, it's Saint Andrew's Night that sets Scots celebrating, at Saint Andrew's town they take their holidays and Saint Andrew's flag they hoist on their kirks and castles.

To judge by documents dated before and after the change from Peter to Andrew, that development took place around 740 A.D. and there are two traditions of how that came to be. Andrew's soul had to wait a long time to hear that he had succeeded Peter, for it had been four centuries earlier that the first of those two traditions had its roots, and that Andrew's name was first linked with Scotland.

Once upon a time around 340 A.D., the first story goes, the good Regulus, Bishop of the Greek city of Patras where the disciple

Andrew was martyred, had a dream that the relic bones of Saint Andrew were in danger from marauders. It had been a happy and faithfully performed task of Regulus throughout his priestly days to guard the precious casket with its three finger bones, a knee-cap, and the arm so often raised in blessing. The dream-teller bade him gather together the treasure and sail from the Greek sea-port, his prow set always for the north. Somewhere, like Paul, he would be shipwrecked and at that place he must set and dedicate a church.

And so, faced every day with the foretold prospect that ill would come to his ship and company, Regulus obediently sailed the seas, bearing northward wherever there was open channel.

After eighteen months a great storm in the German Ocean threw the ship ashore in the lands of Fife with its holy cargo, at a hamlet which the native people called Chilrymont. There Regulus and his little band found a cave for shelter and from that base, sustained by kindly locals, established a tiny church, a resting-place for the martyr's relics. And he called his settlement Saint Andrews.

The second tale starts four hundred years later and not in Greece, but in the north of England in the days when Wilfred was Abbot at Hexham. Wilfred named his monastery there 'Saint Andrew's' from a lifelong veneration for the first-called of all the Twelve, the disciple remembered as the man who brought people to Jesus, the modest martyr who would not share his unique Master's shape of cross.

The story tells that Abbot Wilfred consecrated his holy monas-tery with the relics *he* had brought back from pilgrimage to Patras and that later he passed on his reverence for the bones of Andrew, to Acca the Abbot who came after him at Hexham. Acca added to Wilfred's kist of relics and read in them the true worthiness of the first disciple.

Acca did not sit constantly in pious contemplation or in the monkish comfort of the scholar, he took his staff and script to tra-vel on foot in all directions from Hexham, south among the fells, along the Roman Wall and far to the north across the Tyne River. On one of his journeys he was given hospitality by Angus, then

King of the Picts beyond the Lammer Muirs and the haughs of Tweed and, perhaps to encourage the king in Christian ways, later made a journey to Chilrymont to present him a share of Hexham's holy bones. Tradition does not tell whether King Angus was properly grateful at the moment of the gift, but shortly afterwards he had good reason to bless the Abbot Acca.

It was a time of war and in East Lothian Angus, outnumbered, weary and anxious for his men, faced a great army under the English King Athelstane, who was camped and preparing for battle next day. On his knees at a little prie-dieu in a nearby chapel Angus fell into a fitful sleep and dreamed that he saw Saint Andrew who foretold that his little army would be saved and that the village across the river would not be sacked. Angus woke and raised his eyes, and through the open door saw the sky, blue as a wild hyacinth and streaked with cirrus cloud in the very form of a sloping cross.

Angus took heart from the dream and sky-sign, rose and moved among his soldiers rousing and inspiring them to defend their lands. With new zeal and courage they out-fought Athelstane and won the day. In gratitude King Angus took Andrew for his patron-saint, made the saltire, white cloud on blue sky, the new flag of his lands, and dedicated to that patron a tenth of the possessions which surrounded the settlement at Chilrymont. And he gave the place the name Saint Andrews.

Two traditions from a hundred years apart. . . . Both tales men had known and loved for generations, some preferring one, some the other. But which, if either, was true? Which should be abandoned? Folklore, though, is nothing if not flexible. Men saw truth in both and, undeterred by mismatch of fact and date, wove the two together, altered this and that, brought Regulus forward a few centuries and held Wilfred, Acca and King Angus back. And so one single legend grew round all those actors and events and though it's misted a little in an east coast haar, it tells a good St. Andrews story.

The Apostle Andrew, so it runs, had reached Patras in his mission to 'go out into all the world', and there he preached the Christ and healed the sick. The Governor of Patras ordered death and the only dispensation he allowed was the granting of Andrew's request to die on an X-shaped cross and not using the Master's upright one.

Relics of Andrew were kept secretly at Patras and in time the Bishop Regulus became their guardian. When it was whispered that there was talk of having them stolen away to Constantinople, Regulus had his vision and the voice telling him to journey with the bones to the north.

And then, moving to Scotland, the re-woven story goes on, Angus, King of the Picts had his dream before the battle with Athelstane. In it he met the Abbot of Hexham who told him that Regulus was on his way from Patras with his holy cargo. The spirit of the Saint, he was told, would be with them in the fighting. As sign that this was so the saltire banner appeared overhead in the cloud and blueness of the sky.

Angus made his vow of everlasting reverence for the Saint and for the place where Regulus would make landfall. With his sons the king prepared to welcome him.

In the fullness of time the Bishop came ashore at Chilrymont in Fife, and Angus fulfilled his promise by making a circuit round the site of the landing, dedicating the area enclosed, its pasture-meadows, burns, fertile fields and timber woodland. He gave it in gift to the inhabitants free of tax, called the place Saint Andrews and raised the saltire to be his people's flag.

THE HERITAGE OF
JAMIE CATTENACH

When, around the time of young Jack Cattenach's birth, a Deeside spaewife told his doting parents that the fates dictated he would grow up, for sure, to be clever with his hands rather than with his head. She assured them that she did not mean he would be stupid but only that he would not be a great scholar. His mother and father were well-pleased, for the ungenerous soil of their tiny croft at Burnside called for manual skills and dour physical labour, and would certainly not respond to a mind steeped in Latin or Greek and craving to go away to the University.

Well, Jack grew up with the manual skills, right-enough, but they didn't take the form of dexterity at broadcasting seed, guiding a hand-plough, or of skeely ways with their other simple implements. The lad started to develop his talents early, at feeing fairs or when he went with his father on market days to the small town nearby, for he discovered that his small hands dipped easily into pockets and baskets and came out with all sorts of interesting knick-knacks, and often a bawbee or two as well.

As he grew from child to laddie to hobbledehoy, still practising his secret craft . . . and then into well-put-on youth with a devious kind of charm, Burnside became too small to hold him, for there was no market locally for his pickings that would not have exposed him as a pocket thief. His parents, by now less doting, and anyway with a brood of younger boys more thirled to farm work, were almost relieved to wave Jack off to seek his fortune in the city of Aberdeen, though to be sure it was to 'the fish' or maybe some building company that they expected him to go.

Aberdeen was a small El Dorado to Jack Cattenach. There were busy streets, music-halls, hostelries, markets, and a dozen other locations ideal for his craft. There were seedy men ready and willing to buy his ill-got bric-a-brac; or sometimes he sold them himself from a tray in the old flea-market. He often supposed that if he widened his professional field, to house or shop-breaking, he could be a richer man. But he had his own code and would not have stooped to violence or destruction. He was comfortable enough and by the time he was three-and-twenty he had two small rooms and 'facilities' in an interesting old street near St. Machar's Cathedral, which he attended from time to time (and not only because it was another source of income to him).

All in all Jack Cattenach was quite a happy man. He made occasional visits home to see his parents and to leave them some small sum they fondly imagined he had saved from his sober labour to a satisfied employer. His small home was neat and tidy and he was just about ready to find a wife and settle to family life himself. How he was to get a wife who would thole his trade as an acceptable way of making a living, or who could be hoodwinked into the same misapprehension as his parents, did exercise his mind from time to time. But he was in no great hurry and nursed an optimistic hope that the Lord would provide a suitable mate in due course.

Whether or not the Lord had anything to do with it Jack did find a bonnie wife. They met by kind of accident at the weekly city market, a regular happy hunting-ground for the man who had been born 'good with his hands'. He was in the research phase of his day's programme, eyeing-up the throng for likely prey, rejecting as not being fair game those who clutched their bags and baskets and had to keep counting before they bought; and looking instead for the prosperous who could be slimmed of a purse or wallet, without tragedy.

One of his own victims would never have felt the faint 'stroking' against his hip of Jack's hand in his pocket, but he himself recognised the sensation immediately as a note-case he himself had just stolen to start the day, was gently slid from his jacket pocket. He knew it at once because of being a pick-purse himself and not because it was not skilfully done. He turned quickly, in time to see the curly auburn head of a young woman weaving neatly and purposefully, but not too hastily, away among the crowd. Jack recognised an expert at work when he saw one, and moved after her.

'I think t'maybe I dropped my pocket book back there a whiley. I thocht t'was maybe you t'I saw find it,' he said into her ear as he reached her and put a hand on her wrist. The girl blustered a little at first. But, like Jack, not in her whole career had she been suspected, never mind caught-out, and since she was clearly more upset to think she had been clumsy than that she had been detected in a felony, Jack thought the least he could do was take her for a jar of ale to pacify her.

'Na, na. You mustna think that, I scarce felt a thing and . . . well for a quine to beat Jack Cattenach . . .!' and he explained kindly that it was simply a case of the biter getting bit. 'Really you were grand!'

They got on famously after that, took a spell working the market together and arranged a rendezvous for the next day up Union Street.

And that was it. Two months later they were wed and settled happily in the small house in Old Aberdeen. Nancy made a real home of it, they shared their trade secrets and polished up each other's skills wonderfully well. In time they prospered, moved to a bigger house with a tiny garden and month by month added to their home everything their happy hearts could desire. And then, to fill their cup to overflowing, Nancy knew there was going to be a child.

The birth of their boy (over which the midwife shook her head more than once) brought the very first sorrow to Jack and Nancy Cattenach, for their laddie was handicapped, a sadness in itself, but since the disability took the form of having both hands rigidly paralysed into firm-shut claws it boded ill for his future in the family business, unless the stricken parents could find a cure.

Indeed the only compensation they could discover in their disappointment was that they were now able to afford the search for treatment, and to that search, over the next weeks, the couple committed themselves with great energy. They tried a herb-wife in the country, a seventh son of a seventh son exiled in Aberdeen from the islands, a holy man at St. Machar's, all using their lore, potions, chants and faith, and all failing to unclench the tiny hands. They tried half-a-dozen doctors in the town, who tested muscles, nerves and bones. And then Nancy and Jack went to the cleverest of all the doctor-professors at the University, who approached the problem from a new angle.

'I'm researching, myself, into this kind of trouble . . . that it's maybe a heart or lung problem,' he explained kindly to the distraught parents, and, with his shiny stethoscope dangling over his frock-coat and wing collar he bent over Young Jamie and sounded his chest. Then he made what he thought were funny noises to pacify and amuse a frightened bairn. But it was the glint of the stethoscope swinging before him that attracted the baby's attention. His blue eyes, fixed on it, moved back and forth like his mother's wag-at-the-wa'. Then the two pathetic arms began to inch out from the little body and stretch towards the Professors's instrument. The claw-like hands eased and started to unfold. As the clenched fingers opened and reached for the shiny object, parents and Professor saw a gleam of gold in one little hand and then the gold wedding ring that the midwife had complained of losing when she had struggled to bring Jamie into the world, fell with a tinkle on the floor.

By the time of a return consultation, after a week of gradually increasing waving of arms and waggling fingers, the Professor had decided that his gentle touch on the child's heart and his knowledgeable approach to the matter, had effected the cure, and he had time to add some interesting notes to his research thesis.

Nancy and Jack knew better and chuckled heartily to each other that their Jamie was so much their son that his hereditary skills had operated at the very moment of birth, that he had known to hide his tiny loot and only let go of it when a bigger find seemed to be within reach.

But life is never entirely benign. In his teens, after a visit to his crofting grandparents at Burnside, Jamie took a distaste at the picking-of-pockets and stayed happily there with them to toss hay and plant tatties for the rest of his life. His disappointed parents were left in Aberdeen nursing the hope that, in her turn, his little sister, who truthfully had much less aptitude for the job, would improve on her efforts, with some intensive coaching.

Orkney crofters Mansie Isbister and Christy Hourie were two happy men, for they were all set to wed a pair of bonnie girls who lived in neighbouring croft houses a mile or two from Finstown. The weddings were to be two days apart at the traditionally lucky time of the next 'growing moon'. Tuesday and Thursday were the most propitious days, so Mansie's was for the first of those and Christy's two days later. Mansie was somewhat older than Christy, the brides Kitty and Effie much of an age.

The preparations were well ahead. Usque bottles had been opened between 'grooms and brides' fathers at the official Asking, festivities had been fast and furious on Booking night after the couples' names had been entered in the Session Clerk's papers, the crying of banns was over and the ceremony rehearsed. The fiddlers were bidden, the wedding braws hanging ready, sprigged muslin for the brides, and the navy blue claw-hammer tailcoats and tall hats for the men, outfits that would do them a lifetime of Sundays.

The saga tales of Orkney and the grey, dour weather with its horizon mists, had left a rich legacy of superstitions as to what would bring fair or ill-luck in the days surrounding a marriage and its future. By the 1850s of this tale, Christy and Effie were not much bothered by such notions, nor was Mansie really; but Kitty could tell a thousand tales of the folly of laughing at old wisdoms, and she made her plans with utmost regard for every last whim of the local hogloons.

It was therefore with outrage and incredulity that Kitty and her family heard how, in taking round their word-of-mouth wedding invitations, Mansie and Christy, hospitably well-refreshed at each call, and with superstition the last thing on their minds, had actually asked each other, and their partners, to their respective weddings. For in Kitty's eyes and those of many others in Orkney, to have two same-week brides under the same roof, at either the farm foregathering or the ceremony itself, was to invite the direst of calamities or the most enduring unhappiness on those involved.

In Kitty's family the whole matter was well chewed over . . . among the middle-aged while they set out benches round the barn walls and prepared the wedding food; and among the young fry while they shrieked and guffawed over the ritual washing of the feet of bride and groom. Perhaps just marginally worse than to defy the taboo would have been to withdraw the invitation and hospitality. And so the conclusions from their consultations were that they must just hope that Christy and Effie would have the good sense and caution not to turn up, but that Kitty's uncle who was acting Master-hoosel for the celebrations would deal with them if they were foolish enough to try.

But Christy and Effie had no intention of denying themselves the bere-bread cakes and ale at Kitty's home, for the sake of an old wives' tale, or the pleasure of seeing out the rest of the proceedings as a happy foretaste of their own.

Accordingly they presented themselves in good time at Kitty's place. In fact they were first to arrive and were therefore not greatly surprised when the old uncle told them sheepishly that the barn was not quite ready and would they 'bide a wee while in the chaumer?' Christy and Effie were an accommodating couple and quite happy to be in each other's company in the tiny croft-house where they waited.

And waited. . . .

Meantime the other guests had arrived, seated themselves in the barn, drunk from the ale cog and had a serving of oaten cake and cheese. More than that, the whole company had formed up in twos and, led by bride with best man and 'groom with bride-maid, set out in procession for the manse, a mile away. By the time Christy and Effie, tired of waiting, came out of the cot and hurried after them, Mansie and Kitty had bobbed their little bows of response to the minister, joined hands in wedlock and were now leading the crocodile, behind a piper, back home amidst cheers, laughter and the occasional congratulatory shot from a musket.

It was a fine day for outdoor speechifying, cake-breaking, singing, reel-dancing to Firth the fiddler, and general merry-making. Christy and Effie had sulked a little as they tagged on to the returning procession, but after that they had the wisdom to leave what went on under the barn roof with the older folk, to whom Kitty was showing her dress and the russet shawl that matched her hair. They enjoyed what they could of the rest of the wedding that evening, and its follow-up next day; before, come the Thursday, the festivities began all over again for them.

Whether it was because the niceties had been observed, if only just, both couples lived happily enough for a number of years, and then Mansie, who was senior to the other three by some fifteen years, took a smit, and within a few days died and was laid to rest, beside his Isbister fathers. In another year 'dead bells' (the ringing in the ears Orkney folk heard before a death) tolled for Effie Hourie, who had ailed since the birth of her last bairn. All the invalid gruel, the churn-milk and the tansy infusions in both houses, availed nothing. Mansie's tall hat was put away and Effie's muslin wedding dress, as tradition dictated, became her shroud; and before they were five-and-thirty Christy and Kitty were widower and widow.

What was more natural, after a decent interval, than for a warm-blooded man and a winsome relict to plan a new future together, with their combined broods. And so their wedding preparations were made.

It chanced that a stranger, outdwelling couple came into the community that week, passing time on their way from a visit to one of the other islands, to take the ferry-boat to Scotland. They were warmly bidden to the celebrations, to the assembling in the barn, the ceremony itself and the afterings. All went with a swing and the stranger-pair went off in due course enchanted to have been part of those Orcadian junketings. No one in the village ever saw them again, but it was whispered later that they had been passing through on their way home to Wick where they were to be wed themselves on the coming Saturday.

Now, of those who knew Christy and Kitty Hourie well, half thought them afterwards, a happy well-matched couple; while the other half, who had seen a plate flying or heard an oath from

Christy as he scuttled out of the house into the yard, thought both had chosen better the first time. Those who saw them happy, pooh-poohed the tale that there had been a second bride at the marriage. Those who saw them scolding and out of temper, believed it . . . every word.

The likely truth is that most of the time they were content enough, except when superstitious Kitty was, from time to time, minded of the strangers at their wedding, and taking some silly staw at Christy, flyted him out at the door with her broom, sure that the pair of visitors had blighted her life.

THE PENNY-PINCHER
OF MEARNSKIRK

MacGills had been bakers in the village of Mearnskirk to the south of Glasgow for many generations. Now the baker was Patrick MacGill. Over the years that stretched far back beyond living memory, the family had worked at a succession of ancient primitive ovens, renewing them, either as they wore out, or as new ideas and methods of mixing, yeasting and baking came along. Now, the one that Pate MacGill's great-grandfather had called his 'new foure' was, by the time of Pate's own prime, showing serious signs of wear. He could see that the trouble was the thinning of the stone slab at one end, letting too much heat rise at that side. Increasingly of late, the end of each batch of plain loaves was just a shade darker and crisper than the white softness he prided himself on achieving time after time without fault. He tried less heat, but that made the bread doughy; he tried a shorter bake, but that made it soggy; he tried putting them in on his paddle slightly off-centre, but that made them lop-sided.

Then when three or four of his best customers began to walk to a bakehouse two miles away to buy their bread, he knew it was time to overhaul or replace great-grandfather's 'new foure'.

But Pate was a canny man who would not spend sixpence if a thruppenny bit would do, and not a ha'penny if he could keep it safe in his pocket. The construction of a new oven must, if possible, be avoided and so, too, must a pricey repair. But he knew that at least a new side slab would be needed, and that time was running out. Of course there were merchants in the city who would have come to the bake-house, measured up, then cut and trimmed such an oven-slab and brought it out to Mearnskirk . . . but, and he sweated at the thought . . . only for a wee fortune.

He mulled over his problem for a day or two as he walked, at first light, through the village, behind Mistress Carswell's cottage and past the old kirk beside the bakery. But after producing yet another score of over-baked two pounders that Saturday morning he was making his dejected way home to his breakfast, now facing urgently that massive but essential capital outlay for his oven. That slab filled his mind as he walked. He passed the kirk . . . and then the kirkyard . . . the kirk yard! Over the low wall he saw dozens of slabs! Row upon row of them. All widths, heights and thicknesses. He almost laughed at the thought that struck him. Almost, but not quite.

The village was deserted. So was the kirkyard. Pate louped the wall and walked slowly up and down the overgrown lanes eyeing-up the dimensions of the headstones. He had the grace to restrict himself to the ones that had been weathered nearly smooth of legend, and mentally picked out one that was all but obliterated of lettering, except for the top heading, and which seemed the likeliest for size.

Back at the bakehouse he checked out the size of the oven, and oiled the wheel of his sturdy old barrow. Next morning, never minding that it was the Sabbath, he left home very early, with spade, ropes and two paling stabs that for long enough been drooping loose in his fence.

That day Pate added the sins of Sabbath-breaking and absence from the preaching to those of theft and desecration. But by the time the kirk bell was ringing, the slab that four generations of baking had scorched and worn thin was in the yard and a fine, new, thick side sat firmly in its place. Instead of letting the oven have its day of rest Pate lit the fire and kept up a good red glow to prove the new side ready for the Monday's baking.

There were a dozen startled breakfast-tables in the Mearns that day when the gudewives began to cut their loaves, for, instead of the scorched, crisp ends that had bothered them lately, the texture was soft and the colour near white, but clearly imprinted on the first slice were some of the letters forming the words 'SACRED TO THE MEMORY'.

There were more visitors to the kirkyard during the course of that day than there had been since the last funeral. Most folk came away satisfied that their family headstones still stood safe, but the young monumental mason, Jim Connell, noticed that there was a gap where an old stone from a previous lair of the Connell family had stood drunkenly for many a long year. At first Jim was angry but he was a thoughtful lad and as day succeeded day and it was clear that MacGill had no intention of struggling the sturdy slab out of his oven again, he began to think it something of a sacrament for his family to be remembered in the daily bread of village life.

It's an old story in Mearnskirk and if one similar is told in one or two other places also, that may be because some amused itinerant took it on his travels. But it's surely only some wag's post-script tale that when, in the ripeness of time, Pate passed away just before Hallowe'en one year, and the MacGill gravestone was being prepared for his memorial, the mason's chisel slipped at the date and chipped out 28 oz instead of 28 oct.

THE HANDS OF
MOLLIE-JEAN RANALD

When Mollie-Jean Ranald glanced in the cracked mirror propped against the wall in her bare, off-the-kitchen bed-chamber, she saw, not the bonnie curls she had that were the colour of autumn leaves, not the golden skin, not the clear grey eyes, nor yet her dimpled chin. What she did see, hanging there beside her coarse skirt, was a pair of thick red hands, chapped raw. Those hands were the sorrow and burden of her lonely young life. She turned them this way and that, then she smiled ruefully, put out her tongue at the round face in the old looking glass and took her plaid off the nail on the door. It was milking hour and she couldn't waste time moaning over her hands. She shivered as she crossed the yard that winter morning past the frozen water in the butt and into the draughty byre.

Mollie-Jean was milkmaid and dairy-skivvy at one of the grand isolated houses on the Ardnish peninsula. No one had ever told her that she was pretty. Her parents were long dead, her only brother lost in the wars, and Mistress Niven in the kitchen was a sour woman who would have thought it a dangerous indulgence to risk giving the girl airs by a warm word. The other servants were solid, middle-aged menfolk who lived out, except for two upstairs maids who were indigent kinswomen of the family and therefore part of a different world. And so Mollie had only the young women of the household to compare herself with. They were comely and graceful with fine manners, and when they passed the cowshed on their way to the stables they were laughing and lively and sure of themselves. From head to toe they were goddesses; but it was their pale, soft, beautiful hands that made the girl sore with envy.

It was not that she was jealous of their lives of pleasure. Mollie was quite fond of the cows and of the views she had from the shed, out over the beautiful Atlantic sea. And she had no staw at hard work. Nor did she fancy any of the attentive young men who escorted them; or have ideas above her station . . . no silly romantic notions of catching the laird's handsome heir. Certainly not. For her heart was lost to one she regarded as far superior to any of those. Since she had first seen young Duncan Scott, the piper, when he came, along with his teacher the wonderful Ruari Mhor to play for guests at the big house, Mollie would have snapped her fingers at any other lad.

Ruari Mhor was a famous piper. He could make music that was in turn, tender and wild, haunting and sad . . . music that won him prizes at gatherings all up and down the country from Lochalsh, through the Morars to Sunart. It was said that Duncan's ambition was, not to rival him, but to succeed him and maybe come near in skill someday to one of the most renowned men ever to have blown a chanter.

Molly yearned after Duncan, the crofter's son, for was he not a grand lad, all six feet three inches of him, with eyes like glowing coals and a brown throat that disappeared down into the dark chest hairs curling out between the buttons of his sark? She had never heard him play the pipes, but did not doubt that Ruari Mhor must be shaking in his shoes with Duncan as an up-and-coming player.

But with those hands Mollie was without hope, for even if she had not thought herself too unbraw ever to attract anyone, never mind Duncan, she was not the lass to push herself forward. Anyway he would never look the road she was on . . . but she could dream . . . and peep from behind the dairy door the times he came striding across the stable yard with his mentor, Ruari Mhor, to go and entertain the family. If she was by ill-luck in the yard when they passed, as she had been last evening, she would thrust her rough, red paws into her kirtle and sidle by, with angry tears that she was not more fetching. Those hands . . . those great horrid hands!

In the byre she looked at them miserably as she set down her creepie-stool and luggie . . . with the swollen fingers, thick as the teats of the cow she began to milk. The tears came when she buried her head against the beast's flank and began to pull her udders mercilessly. Then she flyted herself for a self-sorry misery, minding that she had bed and board, her good health and the blue-grey mountains to look at while she worked.

In reasonable weather milking was warm work but on a day like this the freezing wind keening in by the open door chilled her to the marrow and even the new milk did not keep her hands from its biting cut. They grew numb and stiff and as she worked her way along the row of cows they began to shift in complaint at her touch. She sighed, rose and went out to the water butt. She broke the lid of ice with her fist, lifted out a piece and turned it in her hands, rubbing backs and palms until a painful tingling brought them back to life and suppleness.

It continued a bitter winter of frost that year. Even the burns ran narrow between the ice-ing on each side along under the overhang of their banks. Many a morning Mollie-Jean broke the surface of that water butt and deplored her hacked hands . . . but she did not notice the roses that the frost raised in her cheeks.

In spite of the cold, the folk in and around the villages had ceilidhs and weddings, or evenings of friendly gossip over the twirl of rock and distaff. And the big-house people had balls, and wore smart little fur hats, moudie-lined plaids and warm boots to go walking on the ice of lochans or to play the new curling game with smooth dyke-stones. For them the social whirl was at its height in the winter. For the Mollies of the world, those days were usually bleak. But this year her own master was to host an event that would bring cot and big-house folk together in the hall and court-yard for a great piping contest, for all comers from Loch Duich to Morven, to be followed by a barn dance for the plain folk and a banquet-ball for their 'betters'.

More help was taken on for the preparations and Mollie's duties multiplied, to lay tables, move benches and chairs, sweep, dust and shine, and help with the plainer cooking in the kitchen. She caught the excitement and took her customary lonely pleasure in whatever she was doing. The master-piper, Ruari Mhor, would be there and surely, with many more, Duncan Scott too. For there would be no contest if Ruari could not be seen and heard to be far and away the greatest musician among them all, at the reels and waltzes, the dirges and other pibrochs.

The afternoon came cold and sharp but bright, with sun glancing on the frosty cobbles, on the ice on the water butt and the icicles dangling from the eaves, as trails of folk came into the yard from hamlets, isolated steadings, keeps and mansions up and down the countryside. Some stood about, talking and laughing with cronies, some sheltered from the snell wind, at the doors of outbuildings or viewed the scene from upstairs windows.

Mollie looked on from the kitchen door as people stamped leaden feet, blew on their hands and watched the pipers arriving with their supporting groups of pupils, who would fill out the programme without expectation of winning a place.

Then pipes were being tuned up and pipers cheeks blown out like red bladders. Mollie saw Ruari Mhor taking up his position with great presence . . . and Duncan, half a head taller and never heeding for the moment that he was a piper himself, seeing to it that his teacher's chanter and drones were polished up and the tassels hanging untangled, and that distracting youngsters were kept at bay.

There were several competitors before Ruari Mhor, (the likely best being kept for the climax). All of them had some pipe-skill themselves, one this year bidding fair to rival the master. The afternoon grew colder. And then it was his turn. Up went the pipes, he moistened his lips and lifted the chanter. There was a squeal and then a broken blare and a scatter of misshapen notes, as his frozen fingers slipped numbly off the holes.

A hush fell over the courtyard and if there was horror on Ruari's own face, there was anguish on Duncan's, for his master's pride. Ruari handed over the pipes and flailed his arms and hands. But there was no soupling to be roused that way. He clapped them and chafed them but they remained nerveless and stiff. Now Duncan slapped and rubbed them. But it was all to no avail.

There was a stir at the kitchen door. Mollie-Jean stretched up, snapped off a thick icicle from the lintel and darted through the crowd to Ruari Mhor.

'Rub it like soap!' she ordered. Then, impatient with his hesitation to make his hands even colder, she lifted them herself and ran the ice over backs and fronts forcing it between his fingers, scolding him all the time to 'rub it in hard'.

He began to feel the blood rushing into them and the knuckles loosening with seeping warmth. Then he lifted the bagpipes and made no mistake this time. He played like an angel, a virtuoso performance of a marvellous complicated piece that he had spent a month composing for this important day and which was still nameless. He played forlorn and then majestic, and rousing as only pipe music can be. It carried into the hills and valleys skirling and echoing along the rivers. The gathering in the yard went wild.

Loudest applause of all came from Duncan Scott, who himself had come seventh, a healthy placing for him at his age. In his excitement he caught up their rescuer Mollie-Jean, swung her round till her skirts were flying. Then he put her down, planted a kiss on her lips that was sweeter than wine and went to slap his teacher on the back, as the undoubted winner . . . with playing that would go down as legend. Mollie fled inside.

But at the barn dance later Duncan found her and asked her name. At first she kept her red hands behind her back and would not dance. He pulled her on to the floor, then noticed the distress on her face as she tried to tuck them under her arms.

'They're no' fit to be dancing,' she whispered.

'Tis never your hands you dance on, Mollie-Jean Ranald. Tis your feet!'

'But they're so ugly to be showing, held up!'

'Tis a foolish man doesna like to see hands that knows how to work. Look here at my own. My hands is calloused to the bone. I'd be a poor crofter without I had those. Aside from that . . . I canna see your hands for lookin' at your bonnie face.' And he stroked the russet hair, lifted her chin and, with his melting smile made her heart thump in her, like a drum.

So they danced and laughed and fell in love. She danced even with the grateful Ruari Mhor who told her that he now had a name for his winning music and would call it 'The Tune of the Frozen Fingers'.

It was Ruari himself played them to their wedding in the spring and, when eventually over the years his fingers did gnarl up too stiff to play his pipes it was Donald Scott, that he loved like a son, who came to be the new master-piper of Ardnish.

Mollie's hands never were lily-white or dainty, for the work of a crofter's wife was hard. But they were useful. They made a rare home for Duncan and herself, and the bairns they raised never complained when the chapped hands soothed them in fevers, bound up their bruises or ladled out their suppers.

THE BALLAD OF
WILLIE AND MAE-MARGRET

On the south side of the Clyde river, far inland from where it pours itself into the wild Atlantic, there lived at one time a young man who loved a fair maiden from the north bank. It was a long way to the nearest ford and a longer one to the closest bridge. In the early days of their acquaintance, when Willie Forden called on his Mae-Margret, he was content to make the longish hairpin journey and to enjoy his dreams as he jogged along. As his love grew stronger his dreaming was done at a gallop; and when he began to love her so much that he could scarcely bear their days apart, he would throw himself and his coal-black horse into the narowest part of the Clyde, splashing and scrambling his way to Mae-Margret without losing a minute. His lady would watch for his coming and be down at the river-bank to help him to dry land.

They were young, born the self-same day, they were in love and it was their second-fondest dream to run away and be wed the very day they were of age. Their fondest dream would have been to be married by their own priest with bells ringing, wine flowing and both families rejoicing with them. But Willie's mother, the Lady Lilian, had a grander lass in mind for her son; and Mae-Margret's father, a proud tenant crofter, had no time for the Willies of this world, born with silver spoons to their mouths. And neither would budge on the matter by the width of a marsh-rush.

Then the sooth-wife at a market-fair told Willie that she saw in his hand-lines that he was craven in love and would lose his maid from faint heart if he dallied.

'But take care,' she warned him.

That same evening before dining he stood up boldly to his mother and declared that his horse was ready saddled at the stable door to take him to his love and confront her father.

Lady Lilian drew herself up.

'Have I not spoken for you to Mistress Rowena? She's a more fitting wife to mother your heir and my grandbairns.'

'Nonetheless, Mother, it's to Mae-Margret that I go now and will wed when I'm of age.' And he ran lightly down the staircase and round to the stable courtyard. Her voice followed him pleadingly.

'Keep home this nicht, Willie, for I've the best of plump hens for your sup.'

'No fowl will keep me back, Mother. I'm gone before the dark draws in.'

'Tak' tent, William. It's a fell dark night and the wind screams; gin it's mutton you crave I'll bid them kill the finest sheep for your sup.'

'Keep your mutton and your hen, Mother-mine. The wind will but speed me the faster through the river waters.'

'Heed this then, my son, for I swear that an you go, this mother's malison will strike you and your coal-black horse, at the darkest deep of the Clyde.'

'Threttie golden pounds paid I for my coal-black horse, and more faith have I in her, than in your malisons.' And the last she heard was the thunder of hooves.

Over the hill to the river they flew, young Willie and Black Knight, and the closer he came to the Clyde, the greater the roaring made by its waters. Then he saw the swirling black in the darkling night, but his heart was high and his mount was strong. They swam the current and were safe across.

Sodden and chilled but singing, he romped the half-mile to the modest house of his love and loudly chapped the door.

'Open the door, Mae-Margret, for I'm drenched wi' Clyde water and my very boots are full.'

At first there was no answer and then a voice that was surely hers, yet strangely not hers, for it was high and thin and had in it none of the warmth it had always held for him. And stranger yet were the things it was saying.

'Go home, Willie Forden, for I love you not. I have six merry sweethearts here in my chamber and tonight will choose one of them for husband. Go home, Willie Forden. I love you not.'

Willie tried and tried again to woo her to the door, till it was almost dawn. Then he turned away, for she was surely glammered by his mother's curse to have taken other lovers and sent him away. He would go home and charge the Lady Lilian to take back her malediction.

It was near daybreak when he came again to the river which ran more swiftly now and more menacing than last night. Higher than his heart . . . for it was wae and heavy. Horse and man plunged past bent willow and reed, and began the journey across. First the current took his crop and then his plumed hat, which swirled far out of reach.

But Mae-Margret was hard behind him, for she had wakened early, tormented by a dream that she had spurned her dearest Willie at the yett and taunted him cruelly with other lovers. She had roused her father tearfully. He growled.

'Ye think ower much on Willie Forden. He was never here on a nicht like this. He's ower saft-stomached for sic hard a ride. Best back to bed and think to tak' one of your dream-laddies instead.'

But Mae-Margret's dream was too clear, too haunting. She fled the house in but nightgown and plaid. Now she was at the north bank and saw Willie's struggles and the sad plume of his drowning hat.

'Black Knight goes strongly, Willie-love, hold close and swim wi' him,' she cried.

But Willie floundered to catch reins or mane, and even Black Knight's tail he could not grasp.

Mae-Margret stepped into the shallows at the edge, which froze her feet; another step and the waters were at her white knees and with a third, they rose to her throat. Willie was close now. At the deepest bed of the river they clasped hands, then heart to heart. Now Willie minded his mother's curse, as they sank and he knew that his sweetheart was true to him, the cold words of the

Lady Lilian turned instead to benison. For they were together now for ever, he and his Mae-Margret.

OVER THE HILLS
AND FAR AWAY

Sometime early in the years of Victoria's reign Jed Eliot the pedlar, was roaming the countryside and small towns south of Edinburgh, between the Pentlands to the west and the Lammermuirs to the east. He was a popular figure, tall and spindly with flowing black hair under a tammy, a pair of merry brown eyes and always with a red scarf at his throat. Bairns ran to him, menfolk passed the time of day, and enjoyed his crack and the tales of other places he brought with him. Jed was a cheerful man, contented with his lot and sustained by three hopeful ambitions.

One of those was to find a regular call in each of his trading places where he could depend on being given a good meal as a perk, whenever he passed by. He was lucky most places, but on this Edinburgh beat that free sup had always eluded him. Another hope was that someday, before he was old, he would own a good pair of boots; and a third that fate would find him a wife to company with him as he trudged . . . preferably one who owned a good hand-cart.

Those were not burning ambitions, for he had lived near forty years without fulfilling them, but they were pleasant dreams that he nursed as he travelled his patch. He wasn't even thinking about them that March day as he came out of Edinburgh trudging his way in his old bauchles, south through Bruntsfield.

As he took his path by Comiston, Jed met up with a stout middle-aged man coming from the city like himself, but by way of Blackford Hill. He was braw-dressed with snuff-coloured waistcoat and the dandiest boots Jed had ever seen, better even than those of the laird at Whaup's Muir where he often called, or the bien merchant who'd once stopped to buy laces from him. The pedlar always noticed boots . . . and remembered them. The two men matched their strides and chatted a mile or so away, on such things as the fine day it was for March and the busy place the town was getting to be.

'Nairn's my name. Andrew Nairn, exciseman,' the stranger introduced himself civilly . . . 'on my way to John Curdy's distillery at Bowbridge . . . to check his stock, y'ken'.

'I'm Jed Elliot mysel' and I needna' tell you my ain livin'.'

As they got into the slope towards Fairmilehead, Nairn was short of breath and puffing out red cheeks like bladders. So it was a surprise to Jed when, as they reached the village there and topped the hill, the man pulled out a tin whistle and began to pipe up the old tune 'Over the hills and far away'. Jed thought he was maybe a mite odd, or just glad to be on the down slope. Anyway he played well and gave two or three more airs. The pedlar enjoyed the wee entertainment and thanked the gauger for his music.

Jed had known excisemen before. He had also known smuggling, illicit stillers. It was well-enough known that there was never much love between the two parties, but to his mind there wasn't much fondness either between gaugers and proper spirit brewers at local distilleries like the one where this Andrew Nairn was going to calculate the tax due. And so he had a second surprise when they reached the neat-built place at Bowbridge and Nairn greeted the owner warmly, quite in breath again.

'G'day to you, John Curdy. I thought it was time for my measuring visit again.' It was the distiller who was flustered and out of puff now, as he clattered his horse into the yard, having come from some-place by a track that wound out to the south-west.

'Aye man, welcome. You'll step in for a bite after your checkin'?'

Jed tipped his bonnet to John Curdy, thanked the exciseman for his company and took off himself in the Hillend direction where the cart had come from.

As he headed towards his landmark that was Caerketton peak, he found himself following the double tracks that must have been made to and fro, by Curdy's cart. Before he reached the scatter of cots that was Hillend, he came on the broken-down dykes of what had once been a sheep pen. In a corner of it a sacking cover had been thrown hastily over a stacking of casks. A store place was it, that the gauger would be coming to check? There was a wee suspicion niggling at Jed but it was none of his affair and he contented himself with easing out a bung slightly and enjoying the quenching of a thirst he found suddenly on him. It was a warm day for March, the sun was up, the lea side of the dyke was sheltered and, when he had drunk his fill, he slept the afternoon happily away.

Dusk wrapped the countryside when he woke, he took another nip to warm himself up for his journey, put his tent-pack on his back and went his way.

It was a full month before he was that way again, making for Edinburgh. The pen was empty, which was perhaps fortunate, for his pocket demanded that he should be about his business and not dallying to slake his thirst. He did his rounds and as he headed towards Bruntsfield he met Andrew Nairn the gauger once more.

'Am I to hae your company again, sir?' he asked the exciseman.

'I'll maybe make up on you Jed Eliot, but I've a call first that I cannae tell to be long or quick. Go you on, and I'll be behind you.'

Edinburgh never gave Jed much to jingle in his pouch and he wasn't sorry to leave the place behind, so he nodded and set off again, turning round once or twice as he took the long slope up over Fairmilehead, to see if Nairn had appeared. Then the pedlar dropped towards the distillery at Bowbridge which lay quiet in the April sunshine. When he reached it Jed sat on a boulder by the burn, hidden from the buildings by an alder tree. He had just delved into his pack for the day-old slab of bread and sliver of cheese that was all his 'business' in Edinburgh afforded him, when the piercing notes of 'Over the Hills' floated down from Fairmilehead.

Immediately all was clamour here at the distillery. A horse backed into cart shafts, there was the thump and clatter of barrels on to carts, the hoisting up of a hardy-looking maidservant in apron and shawl to keep them from falling off and the opening of the gate by a lad. Then John Curdy leapt up with the reins in his hands and the cart was lumbering away noisily down the track to Hillend.

Jed thought he was alone at the distillery at first. He dipped his bread in the burn and drank from it thoughtfully, putting two and two together as he supped. There had been that quiet calm when he arrived here, the sudden whistle . . . and then the exodus, soon there would be the arrival of the gauger. He walked round the building. The dwelling house was onbuilt to the distillery and through a winnock he could see a woman, maybe Mistress Curdy, setting out a grand table with beef and pickles, thick scones with the steam still rising on them, then bottles and a dish of fruit. Jed went back to the boulder.

Soon, as if it was timed from long practice, John Curdy arrived back, breathless as last time, just when Andrew Nairn in his snuff-coloured weskit and fine boots turned into the yard.

'Welcome Gauger Nairn, sir. I'm pleased I didnae miss you. I was on an errand to my kinsman, Hillend-way,' said the distiller.

'You got your deliveries made safe then?'

'Aye, aye. You'll can dae your tottin' up just whenever you like. But you'll dae us the honour of eatin' wi' us first, will you no'?'

Jed stepped out from behind the elder, threw the last of his crust to the chilfies and came up from the burn.

'Your business didnae tak' you that long in the town, gauger, but I'm sorry I didnae hae your company,' he said cheerfully to Andrew Nairn.

'It's yersel', Jed Eliot. Meet Master Curdy here, the distiller at Bowbridge.'

'Pleased to meet you, sir, beyond the nod we 'changed last time. But I maybe made the acquaintance of your spirits a'ready when I took a wee taste, out Hillend there. I must ask your pardon for that, but I was fair parched,' said Jed easily, his head to one side, eyes sharp on the two wary faces before him.

The distiller coughed.

'Will you no' step inside and join us in a bit-meal, Jed Eliot . . . that's richt is it . . . Jed Eliot?'

Over their food the three did broach the subject of a small purse of hushing-money, but Jed knew his own ways and weaknesses, and that any lump sum would trickle through his fingers, like the burn there, in just a week or two; but neither had he any taste for ongoing blackmail. He could make a more practical investment.

'Nae money atween friends, I think, masters. But y'ken, I've a fancy for a pair boots no unlike your own there, gauger.' Nairn nodded and bent down.

The pedlar turned to John Curdy. . . . 'And gin I might just refresh mysel' at your table, or even your kitchen, when I come by this way, sir . . . no more'n once-twice a month . . . I would take that a kindness.'

Jed had had a good look round. There was something else that he had his eye on, two things really, but they could wait.

He went off that day, comfortable in his wame and soopling happily along in the soft leathers, better shod than ever in his life before. He would remove the boots presently, sling them over his shoulder to walk on the easy moors, and keep them to wear on town ruts and cobbles.

All in all, gauger and distiller thought they'd got out of the matter quite well, when weeks passed and Jed Eliot made no further demands on them than his meat in the kitchen, an odd nip of spirits and a scrape of polish for the boots once in a while. Another man might have insisted on being served along with the master and mistress in the good room, but then he would not have had Annie-the-maid's company. Three times he'd called now. He liked her wiry looks and her pawky chat the better for every visit.

'Dinnae much like bein' in service. I'm fae down Tweedside afore here. Half-gipsy I am, my faither was fae Yetholm,' she said proudly.

'What brought you this way?' asked Jed.

She laughed. 'Seekin' my fortune maybe.'

'You didnae find it then?' She ladled him out another bowlful of broth and looked him over.

'I'm no sure aboot that,' she said slyly.

So that was how two-and-a-half of Jed's heart-desires were met.

And he made it up to three when he saw the distiller in the yard, the day he came for Annie.

'Yon hand-barrow 'gainst the shed wall, Master Curdy, you wouldnae think to give Annie and me that, for a weddin' gift?'

The distiller nodded. The truth was that, though Annie was a happy lass, she was a wee-thing slap-dash for his lady-wife and Jed was taking her away with their blessing, so the old hand-cart was small price to pay. She would be fine and happy, they were sure, trampling the tracks alongside the pedlar, pushing the barrow with their gear in it; while at Bowbridge they would look for a town-bred servant-girl.

Curdy and his wife waved them out of sight promising to have a sup for them both whenever they came by. Then suddenly, from the north, behind them, came the high notes of 'Over the Hills' from the gauger's whistle. The distillery sprang to life and action. Curdy ran back and pushed out the cart, his wife led the horse from the field, the bung-boy louped the wall and ran to fetch out some of the casks from the store.

By the time Jed and Annie were out of sight to the south, the empty cart was halfway back from the pen at Hillend, and all that remained of stock at Bowbridge was what Nairn would see when he reached the distillery, righteously count and tax accordingly.

THE PARLEY AT THE LOCH

Deterrents are not new, neither is negotiation nor verification. In the lands of the West Highlands they knew the tactics, if not the words, as far back as the 15th century.

Away beyond the wooded lands skirting Loch Rannoch a mile or two past its western end, lies the little Lochan of the Sword, steel-grey when the clouds are low, and jewel blue in sunshine. It was once called locally Three-Heart Water, for it was reckoned that three great shires met together in the middle of the loch, Argyll, Perth and Inverness. But that was long before the incident which gave it its 'new' name, five hundred years ago.

Around the shores of the lochan lay Cameron land and also Athol country and since the early days of clan history the exact running of their boundaries had been in dispute, moving back and forward like the tide, depending on the relative strengths at any given time of the two clans. It was, for instance, a matter of pride to the Camerons in one generation, when their chief was strong enough to stake claim to an extra mile or so of land, to fish its burns and graze their cattle, or even lay claim to Athol animals, declaring that they had strayed on to Cameron land and were therefore confiscate. Then in another generation an Athol chief would be some great wight with a flailing sword, a voice of thunder and a will that brooked no nonsense from a Cameron. The bounds would be pushed back behind cattle or crop, and the current Cameron would bow to this strength, relinquish the territory and wait for reversal of power.

At the time of this tale it happened that for once the Athol chief and the Cameron of Lochiel were men well-matched in valour, guile and even some little honour. They had come into their inheritances at much the same time and, in the early days when they were taking the measure of each other, Lochiel would lead a party out with him and set forward a stretch of the boundary boulders a trial twenty-five yards. The next day Athol would reply, riding down with a group of his men and setting them back, not just the twenty-five yards, but fifty. Then it was a swing of seventy-five yards, then a hundred each way. When the two men chanced on the area at the same time they glowered across the lochan, neither moving away until it was dark. It seemed as if dourness on both sides would eventually break into temper and bloodshed.

Now there was one inhabitant in a safe little corner of that disputed land, a small weathered woman, hardy and squat as a garron pony, who claimed no kinship with either tribe. She liked fine to see the clans at loggerheads and the shifting ownership of the land back and forth, because in the tulzie of wills, when neither side knew what was whose, she could filch some of the crops in season and lead the odd beast into her own little yard for private slaughter. These she sold to a small settlement where some of the Menzies clan lived, on a finger of land jutting between Athol and Cameron territories. With them she conducted a sly and lucrative little trade, primed solely by the rivalry of the other two clans.

It was therefore a matter of some worry to old Mhaire when, as she was gathering firewood by the lochan one fine day she met Col, the drover, who gave her some disturbing news.

'They're to make peace, Athol and Lochiel. Coming here to the shore, both of them, to parley . . . just the one to one . . . about fixing their dykes for sure; for they're weary of the thieving of land and beasts.'

'Parley . . . one to one!' She had never heard of such a thing between Camerons and Athols. 'When?'

'They're saying, back there at Rannoch that it's to be at dawntime after the next full showing of the moon. That's maybe six-seven days away,' said Col.

Mhaire was abroad early, before daybreak, the day after the next full moon. She found it necessary that morning to gather her herbs and dye-plants, first of all round the home of Cameron of Lochiel. She wandered into a spinney close to his horse-yard, lurking there until the Chief himself came out. The old woman was tolerated there as harmless, as in most places, useful for herb remedies, and relied on for a small gift she had of the second sight.

'There was warning for you in my dreams last night, master,' she said, putting a hand on his plaid. 'I saw you by the lochan shore waiting for another . . . waiting, waiting, and alone by yourself. Then I saw the man come, but he was not alone. He had men with him. I can't say the meaning of such a dream, master, but I smelled danger.'

She left Cameron pensive and a little angry. The bargain with Athol was that each would come to the meeting-place unarmed and alone. Now it seemed Athol was to break his pledge. He went to seek out a party of some fifty of his men.

Meantime Mhaire had hurried to meet Athol and give him the

same spiel. Athol too was roused at Lochiel's going back on his solemn word and, lining up twenty of his clansmen to hide in the heather behind him, made his way well ahead of them, to the loch.

Lochiel, his men carefully concealed behind tussock and heather clump, reached the western shore of the Three Hearts Lochan that cold dawn, and stood on a skirting of shingle beside the lapping water. Then he saw the sturdy figure of Athol approaching, alone . . . no sign, as Mhaire had said, of a party of followers. There was shame in Cameron at the thought of his men in the heather behind him, grimly ready for trouble.

Because of his shame, Lochiel was the more courteous in his talking with Athol, a taciturn man, not much used to manners and patience. The bargaining for a yard here, or a patch contained in a loop of a burn there, went on for some time between them, with Lochiel intent on being fair after his suspicions. Athol began to think he had misjudged the Cameron chief, and decided that Lochiel was an easier opponent than he had thought. His requests and requirements became more and more demanding until it seemed that half-a-mile too much of Lochiel's land was to be dyked away to Athol. Cameron started to growl, his courtesy roughened, and soon there were high words and threats flying.

Then Athol lifted a signalling hand and twenty men leapt out of the heather. At once Lochiel flashed the scarlet lining of his cloak and fifty Camerons rose as one, from the slope behind him. At a glance Athol took in the disparity between twenty and fifty, threw back his head and laughed so that the echo resounded across the lochan. Then he drew a basket-hilted sword from under his cloak, raised it, kissed the blade and pitched it far into the middle of the lochan.

'I declare in honour that I renounce my claim to this half-mile stretch of ground, and that so long as this sword lies in the loch, the land is that of Cameron of Lochiel.'

Old Mhaire had been stymied by her own double-dealing. There was no more corn or cattle thieving, for title to the land was firm now and everything on it was tallied. But she was a kenspeckle body in those parts, learned in herbs and salves, and neither party would have seen her starve. There was ale and brose from the Athols, meal and marts from the Camerons, as long as she lived.

Lochiel had acknowledged the swearing of Athol's vow that day, by sending his own previously hidden dirk after the sword, but had watched carefully afterwards for any sign that the other chief would try to recover his weapon and thereby retract his promise. But he never did and, in the matter of the boundary at least, peace reigned thereafter in Rannoch.

In 1826 one tremor did run through the lands which still belonged to the Camerons and Athols at that time. A young lad fishing from a small boat in the Lochan of the Sword, reeled-in the rusted sword caught by the hilt in his hook. He had hoped for a fat trout for his supper, but this was even better. At home, his father turned the sword over once or twice, then took it down with him to the inn.

Every evening by that time there were Atholl men and Camerons both, warming themselves round the fire with drink and good chat; and a new barman would never have known which were which. But they'd all been reared on the folk tale of the loch, and by the time a few jugs of ale had been emptied the land alongside Jimmy Cameron's barn and stretching up to the far burn, was being as hotly disputed as in the 1400s, and now that the sword was out of the water a melée seemed imminent.

It was maybe fortunate for the peace of the community that the minister of the day was a man who whiles liked his dram at the inn. That one dram was all he took and his head was cooler than most. Besides he was a lowland man with no axe to grind. He put down his glass, took the sword solemnly and with dignity, bore it out of the pub and down to the lochan, followed by a scrambling, arguing crowd. Then he raised it as high as the old Athol had done, flung it out into the water, listened for the splash and turned to his flock.

'Noo, you can just all plant your 'neeps where you've aye planted them and give over battling old wars like you were savages. Yon Cameron Lochiel and the Chief Atholl had more sense than the pack of you.' He bade them goodnight and marched back home to his manse.

And there in the water the two blades still rest and the sun rises and sets peacefully on the shores of the Lochan of the Sword, as it has done these many years.

FAIR WINDS TO FORTUNE

Clever men know that the stone-using people who lived on the Hebrides in times long past were very small of stature. They know that, because the bones unearthed there are far shorter and more slender than those found of the warriors who conquered them. Those later men were the Nordic marauders who came to take their land and subject them with terrifying iron weaponry and implement. When, in after years, the small folk wedded with the tall newcomers the generations of their sons and daughters stood in height somewhere between the two. In time, memories that there had even been short men and women of the islands became blurred . . . shifted and drifted from fact to legend, and settled into the fanciful belief that in some sub-world of the Hebrides, there still lived and breathed a race of Little People, making their homes in humplocks and knolls, coming out by night and early morning to communities of ordinary mortals, to do them good or ill, according to their merits and their treatment of the knoll-folk. It was as good an explanation of the vicissitudes of life as any other. The fear that their less sturdy island ancestors had had for the metal blades and axes of the tall Viking muscle-men, came down as further lore that the fancied Little People were helpless before the appearance of ironware, from whatever quarter it came. Thus their folk-speak abounds with tales of the fairy-folk, and their adventures against the threat of cold iron . . . like this one of the surly island farmer who was the butt of many Little People mischiefs.

He was a man with few friends. Even his bonnie daughter had left home for service in a happier household, after a quarrel with her father over a fisher-lad called Adam, who wanted to marry her. The farmer swore that so poor and happy-go-lucky a boy would never have his lass.

'You'll tak' the first man t'offers t'has a bag of silver coins to show,' he declared firmly. And that was the mean, joyless man known to neighbours and Little People alike.

Other crofters put out bits of bannock for the Little People, small bowls of oatmeal swirling with cream, and scraps of fine tweed to make coats and caps against the dank cold inside the knolls. Those good folk were much too kind too, ever to disturb such hummocks, even though they had to draw aside their foot-ploughs to avoid them. They were rewarded with bunches of flowers, the almost invisible mending of torn clothes they had left lying, and with offerings of fat mice for their cats. But the farmer in this story scraped his coggie clean of brose, ate even his dry crusts, wore his old clothes into rags, and cared not a jot whether he flattened or tore open knolls that were in the path of his heuk.

'Pshaw . . . Little People . . . never such n'a thing!' He scorned those who took tent of their traditional elves. But the others knew fine that even if he had thought the fairies existed he would have been just as mean with his left-overs and his sickle.

The Little People were angry at not being believed in, and began a campaign of naughty ploys to challenge his doubts. At night they would come by and sour his cream or pull the roots of his crops deep underground; they coggled his milking-stool and tied the tails of his goats together; they bored holes in his meal girnal and on cold nights tweaked the very bed-clothes off his feet.

After a spell of this (and that word was beginning to loom large in his mind) he began to wonder whether perhaps he had been wrong and that there were indeed Little People upsetting his life. He wondered privately, for he would never have admitted such a thing to his neighbours, and then, after finding the handle of his peat-spade buttered and slithering about useless in his hands, he was sure of it.

A more sensible man would have mended his ways and been granted the favours of the Little People that others in the parish enjoyed. But that was not John Surly's way. He fumed and ranted, then thought of the traditional distaste his tormentors had for iron, and planned a terrible revenge for their pranks. He took his old sickle-hook and went searching for the tussock near his land where folk said the Little People lived, and he curled the blade far round into the earth, until the whole curve, and half the handle, were buried, so encircling the knoll with iron and imprisoning the occupants. If he heard low squeals of fear, he paid no heed but marched off with a grim snarl on his face.

For weeks, not a posy lay on a kitchen step, not a rent sark was mended, tabbies went without mouse-gifts and good folk were sad to think that their little friends had deserted them.

Now just when the parish had quite given them up for lost, it happened that Adam the fisher-lad with the brown curls, who loved the farmer's daughter, was blown ashore in a wayward wind. He landed near the hamlet and although he should have been downcast at losing the day's fishing, he decided to make a happy best of matters and walk over to visit his sweetheart. He would find her in her mistress's kitchen a mile or two inland up a sloping track and ask if her stern father had relented yet. It chanced too that, having been buffeted by sea-winds and then had to beach his boat, he was tired enough to sit down before he started the climb. As luck would have it, where should he sit but on the mound of the imprisoned Little People?

At first, from the throb under his rump, he thought that he had sat on an ant-hill, but he had never heard-tell of ants whimpering and sobbing, and realised that this, for sure, was an elf-knoll. Then he noticed the heuk handle and pulled it free to see just what it was. At once, as the gird was removed, there was a sigh of relief like wind in sedge-grass, and a torrent of Little People came rushing out, dancing, singing and shouting with glee. Hither and thither they dashed, trying out their legs again and drawing in great gulps of fresh air. Then they remembered their manners and crowded round to praise and thank Adam for saving them.

'A gift!' they cried. 'You must have a fine gift from us. Choose, choose!'

'I need no gifts, for when I have a home you will befriend me there.' But they would not be gainsaid.

'No, no . . . a gift, a gift!' they chanted. 'I know,' said their chief at last, 'we will give you the best of presents for a sailing man.' Ceremoniously the little fellow drew himself up to his full height and declared solemnly, 'May you always have God's breath in your face.'

Adam nodded equally solemnly, for he was a good-natured lad and, although he was chuckling inwardly at such a fey, fanciful and useless benison to have as a gift, he thanked them politely, told them he was happy to accept and glad to have done them a good turn. Then he said good-bye and set off cheerfully up the slope, still laughing to himself at their idea of a gift.

He had a happy hour with his Ishabel, but it was spoiled as ever by hearing again of her father's thrawn insistence that her husband must be a rich man. But now the wild sea had quietened and he set off back to his small boat, wondering with every step how he would ever win Ishabel, and yet with a smile breaking into his rueful thoughts at the queer gift of the Little People.

But in the days that followed he found that their offering was not so strange at all . . . for a man with his living to make with a boat it was a boon of the greatest usefulness. He quickly discovered that he had but to change his place aboard to have the wind blow from wherever it would best speed him to the shoals of silver darlings. Every day his catch for selling was greater, and of better quality, than any other fisherman's and the counting of his coins a longer job. Soon he had earned enough to buy a bigger boat with a wider sail and was able to start a little trade, fetching and delivering goods up and down the coast, flying like a bird among the islands with breezes from whatever direction he cared, to fill his sail.

Before the winter solstice he was able to come to the surly farmer's house, throw a bag of silver coins on the kitchen table and claim Ishabel for his own wife. The old man may have been glumshie and cantankerous but his word was his word and he agreed to the marriage. He did so with bad grace at first but his manner thawed with every second, as he saw the money counted out and realised that Adam was now in the way of real prosperity.

The farmer never became a favourite with the Little People but as he grew older, his grandchildren warmed the cold core in him, and he began to offer the elves tit-bits of this-and-that on his doorstep. And they, in their turn, left off teasing him and turned their attention to the miller's new wife over the hill, a bad-tempered churlish young woman from another island, who needed to be tormented into better ways.

THE TWO CRIMES AT ALVIE

It was maybe because times around the aftermath of the 'Forty-five were so dark and brutal, and because so many in the north-east never came home again after Culloden, that there was not more furore over the disappearance about that time of a pedlar from somewhere in the area of the parish of Alvie. It was thought unlikely that he was the victim of official violence for he was neither a known Jacobite, nor one who would have supported Charles Edward's enemies. A man who was quite loud in his insistence that the pedlar had likely been a redcoat spy and had been done to death by angry clansmen somewhere, was the crofter Marcus Grant, a cantankerous man who was not much liked in the small community. But few believed that theory, for the packman's life had been in small wares and he had been a welcome sight to folk in cots and castles, no matter what their politics, whenever he appeared.

Of course he could just have taken to a different patch for his rounds and found new customers, and Marcus Grant the farmer admitted that that was a possibility. But most dismissed that too, for he was an old friend and did well around Alvie with his trinkets and household goods. So well, in fact, that he was known to have been carrying a good week's takings when he left his last call, to make for his home hamlet before the coming Sabbath. And therefore, although he was never found and it was never proved that he had died, there was a general suspicion that foul play for his money, had befallen Chay the packman. His disappearance was a matter of regretful gossip for a week or two, and then parish clash moved on to other matters and by the time of the next part of the story, twenty years had passed and only the middle-aged and old remembered anything about the incident.

One early autumn day, those two decades later, another traveller came into the district, but not a known pedlar. This time it was a shepherd, a stranger to those parts, driving his sheep across Feshiebridge at a rather pacier rate than the usual drifting amble of herds across that rough ground. Now it happened that the only other man on the landscape that morning was Marcus Grant, older, plumper and a little more prosperous than he had been in the days when he was so sure that the last pedlar had been either a redcoat spy or had left for a new beat and clients. Grant had come on a path from the west and his way was about to converge with that of the shepherd. The herd approached him.

'Can you show me, Farmer, the way to the old drove road they tell me goes through the Rothiemurchus forest?'

'I'm bound that road myself. I'll go part-ways with you and get you on to the right track a mile or two ahead.'

Those who had known Marcus a long time might have thought he was looking for a shilling for his troubles, for he had never been a man to trouble himself much to do a kindness to anyone.

It seemed to the crofter that the shepherd did not altogether trust him to know the direction, for the man kept turning his head nervously to look back the way he had come as if wondering if he should have peeled off along some previous path.

It was a fine morning. The countryside was bonnie, the air soft and still but for the murmur of the two as they walked and the grey wave of the sheep moving in front of them. Then, as their path drew level with an area of woodland, from far behind them, the men heard the sound of horsemen. They glanced round. The herd's eye darted towards the wood.

'I havena broken my fast the day and I see a bush of fine berries there among yon trees. Will you do me the kindness to keep by the sheep while I find myself a handful o' brambles? The animals are going on sweet and I d'na want to stop them. I'll make up on you,' and the herd thrust his crook at Grant and slipped into the shade of the trees leaving him no choice but to follow the flock.

The crofter shook his head as he went forward. He was trying his hand at the herding with a touch to the rump of a straggling sheep when the close thunder of hooves startled him and he found himself separated from the sheep, by the prancing of two horses reined in suddenly in front of him . . . the animals and riders they had noticed some way behind five minutes earlier.

'Villain, stand you still, for it's been a long time to catch wi' you and no' a step further are you going!'

Grant's face was grey as putty and the sweat of fear was on him.

'I'll come, I'll come wi' you . . . just d'na shoot.'

One of the men frowned and leapt off his mount.

'Coward too, are ye? Afore you've as much as seen a pistol!' The crofter shivered and his voice came from a tight throat.

'It's been that long. I've lashed in fear these twenty years that this hour would come on me.' The captor scratched his head.

'You're in an offa state, man . . . what's this about twenty years? Twenty minutes, more like, since you stole the sheep.' But, too loudly to hear him, Marcus Grant was babbling admission of much worse than sheep reiving.

'I confess . . . I confess . . . Chay the pedlar had a fat purse o' money. I knifed him and never a minute's peace I've had since-ever that day. You'll find his bones yonder by the birk wood past the river. Just put up your weapon and d'na shoot, and I'll come wi' you.' And he held out shaking hands for a rope.

One of the horsemen obliged and when Grant was safe-trussed and ready to go where they would find someone in town who would know better what to do with him, the puzzled captor, voiced his query.

'So you are telling us it's murder's your crime, shepherd . . . along wi' the sheep stealing? You were offa quick wi' your confession for we were after no more 'n the two sheep you took of us this very morn . . . and maybe one of your own for a bit of interest on the "loan".'

'But I'm no' the shepherd at all. I was but bearing him comapny and mindin' the sheep while he berry-gathered in the wood there,' wailed Marcus.

In due course of hauling before the authorities in the city, of seeing the grisly remains of poor Chay Packman dug up, then of trial and sentence, Marcus Grant, the crofter, was to hang for his crime. But twenty years of gnawing conscience, fright at being rounded up by the horsemen at Alvie and the ghastly prospet of dangling from a gibbet, brought on a fatal heart-seizure before ever he left his cell.

As for the sheep-stealing shepherd who had jouked into the wood, he got off with a cuff on the ear when he was dragged out that fateful day. That, with the removal from him of the rustled sheep and two of his own for good measure, and the ordeal of having to appear as witness at the trial, was enough for him.

He didn't much like any of those experiences and was careful to mend his thieving ways in the future.

THE BLACK BEADS

Cars and jewellers and business trips don't seem the stuff of which folk tale or legend are made. Yet future generations will surely look as much to the 1900s for their lore as to the 1500s, and there's a tale they tell in Lanark that draws those two centuries together.

They swear in museums that it's not true and give half-a-dozen cogent reasons for being so sure, but the story persists all the same.

In the days of the 1930s when a motoring trip was a treat (and not just a hurtling from one place to another) a city man from Edinburgh, who had business in Lanark, took his daughter with him for the day out: He gave her a little money to spend while he was about his affairs. Kate Nimmo window-shopped in the High Street, bought a cream cotton shirt and fingered the corner of it happily while she drank a cup of tea in the baker's shop next door. From there she could see a small antique shop across the street and decided to challenge herself to finding some trinket costing no more than her remaining pound.

The shop bell rang as she entered and a little man, brown and smooth as a hazelnut, showed her a tray of what he called 'objets' where she could rake for a find. There were broken buckles, medallions, thimbles and tarnished tea spoons, one with a golf-ball topping the handle . . . but she decided that it was beads she was after, something to go nicely with the cream shirt. She moved to a rack of necklaces. There were amber ones too dear, wooden ones that were dull, and red ones too short for the neckline. And then the little man tugged open a drawer, rummaged in it for a moment and brought out a string of dark beads . . . good length, perfect colour with the cream . . . and only ten shillings and sixpence . . . exactly right. The clasp was loose but they had a nice lustre (unless it was dust), and the bric-a-brac jeweller at home in Morningside could fix that.

She bought her father the golfball teaspoon and joined him for lunch.

Next day Mr. Nimmo took his daughter's beads to their local jeweller.

'Can you put a new catch on this string of beads for Kate, McMurtrie?' McMurtrie rubbed them up with a duster.

'Nice,' he murmured . . . 'nice.' He knew Nimmo as a prosperous business man but he was a canny Scot too, and these seemed a little unlikely for a young lass like Kate, who normally favoured three-and-sixpenny brooches.

'You wouldna sell them to me?' he tried. Nimmo was curious.

'How much?'

'Mm . . . hundred and fifty.' Nimmo was also shrewd.

'I think not. The lassie has a fancy for them. They're not mine to sell anyway.'

'Tell her, though,' persisted the jeweller.

'Aye, I will. But never heed the clasp then, till I see her.'

Nimmo was in London on business later that week and took the beads, now wrapped in a silk handkerchief, into Charterhouse's, a jeweller in Bond Street. A startled young man there asked his name and called the senior partner. Mr. Nimmo was invited into the back office and offered coffee. The senior partner had his glass at his eye, peering.

'An heirloom, Mr. Nimmo?' he suggested. The tale of the day-out to Lanark was told, but not that of the Edinburgh jeweller.

'If you thought them only a string of beads, what brings you here?'

'I've an idea they're maybe some better than that,' replied the Scotsman.

'They're black pearls.' Nimmo digested that.

'Rare?' he asked.

'These ones are unique. And they've been lost a long time,' said the jeweller.

'You know something of them then?'

'Well, I don't know where they've been since . . . when was it . . . about 1586 or 7? But I do know where they were prior to that.'

Mary Stuart's prison chamber at Fotheringay Castle was draped with black and there were other mortifications arranged in anticipation of the morrow's execution. Her petitions to Queen Elizabeth remained ungranted and she grieved sore that her son King James of Scotland was so little moved at her fate. She was now spending the eve of her death talking quietly, weeping and praying with her faithful intimates and distributing some of her cherished treasures among the ladies who lovingly supported her, and to the gentlemen who attended her to the last . . . a picture of her beloved and unloving son, pieces of her own exquisite embroidery, miniatures, hair ornaments, her coral necklaces, pendants and a jewelled phial of sweet perfume. She looked long at Bothwell's jet ring and even longer at her black pearls. When she was young, in the brief days when she had danced and held court and gloried in the world, she had loved them for their dramatic contrast to her white skin. Now she saw them differently. They were for death and she would have them round her neck tomorrow . . . her neck . . . she touched it and felt the quivering pulse of dread at her throat. Then when she saw little Lady Cristian Hogg break down and weep again, she closed her casket and put an arm of comfort round the girl. Her own only compensation was to make herself believe that she would die a martyr to the True and Holy Church.

The night passed with bathing, grooming and anointing, and the slipping on of cambric, velvet and silk, the black pearls, the crucifix of gold. Finally, in the early morning the auburn wig that in those latter days turned her from ageing, greying woman to elegant Queen, was gently laid over her ill-fated head and topped with a lace winged cap.

On that winter morning, disabled by years of poor health, she was supported into the Great Hall at Fotheringay where a platform had been raised that was higher than the six feet she had stood as a young woman. She climbed the steps, sat on a bench to listen to her sentence, then touched her rosary, said a last few words of prayer, commendation and farewell; and knelt down before the saddle in the block. Her eyes were bound, she witnessed finally to her Faith, took the hands of the first executioner and waited for the axe of the second.

Afterwards there was a swift gathering up of body for burial, small clothes, draperies and accessories for disposal and, it's said, even the taking away of a tiny dog who had hidden under Mary's skirts, her last companion. Her rings, her chains and holy crosses were collected by the executioners and handed over . . . all except the black ring and death pearls she had thought fitting last ornaments, which were lost, from that day, to royal collections or interested antiquarians. If the pieces went into the pouches of the executioners, as people say, perhaps they saw their takings as no more than loot . . . but maybe they reverenced them as precious mementoes of a tragic Queen.

Tradition does not say where the first executioner lived in later years, but it does insist that the second, weary of his calling, went back home to Scotland to live out the rest of his days by the River Clyde in his own native town of Lanark.

Note: Perhaps the experts are right and that if the black pearls had indeed come into the hands of reputable jewellers they would surely have ended up in some museum of antiquities or part of one of the great collections . . . unless, of course young Kate Nimmo, whoever she was, refused to part with them and they are lost for four more centuries or longer.

KAIL RUNT AND BARN DOOR

Every year by Hallowe'en time, there was a clutch of mainland Orkney lads and lasses ripened ready for marriage since the year before, and looking for sign-posts to the future. The younger ones may have played the guessing games for fun, but those just flowering went through the rituals solemnly. The simple ones believed it all; the clever ones not a bit of it . . . so they said.

Sara Flett despaired of ever finding a lad. Her friend Gerda was small and slim, had a sleek cap of dark hair, and chin and eyes like an elf . . . enchanting. Sara, in contrast, was new grown this last year, and didn't know what to do with her arms and legs. She was tall, big-boned and ruddy, with hair the colour of nothing more exciting than gold barley. She had also a wide, shy smile and no idea at all that she was beautiful . . . 'a corn-marigold' the mester had thought a time or two when he had turned sadly from looking at his own white, ailing wife.

It startled Sara therefore on that witch-and-warlock night of

Hallowe'en that when she and Gerda and a handful of others went out on the moonless night to pull kail runts and see from their shapes what form of life-partner they were to have, she pulled up a well-proportioned plant that told of a handsome man . . . a plant with half-a-dozen bud-knots that tokened six bairns in her home. Yet Gerda, neat and pretty as a velvet moudie, drew a root thin as a bere stalk that meant a sleevin, a skinny boy, with only one pair of buds that said he would give her but two babes.

'Truth!' thought Sara, 'wir hands has surely got mixed in the dark.'

But when they 'cast' the glasses later, in the henhouse, it was the same story. They filled the tumblers with water, separated egg-whites into them, and watched. Hew Phin, who fancied himself as forespeaking what the shapes said, told her that the gainly composing of her egg-white meant that she would wed a good, kind, man, lordly and strong as a Viking. Gerda's egg, on the other hand, took shape like a thin stem, straight up and down in the water. 'A sleevin, right enough,' said Hew.

It was hard to believe, and Sara was inclined to agree with the free-thinking village carpenter that it was all moonshine: until a month later Gerda told her happily that she was to wed one of the young fisher-lads down the shore, skinny-lean and straight as a reed in his navy jersey, not tall but just-right for size with Gerda, and well-matched in spirit.

Sara was maid-of-all-work on one of the grander farms in the parish. She had no parents and was fond of the family there. The mistress's breath came sore on her these days and it was as much as she could do to turn spurtle in pot. Sara was strong and willing, the bairns were biddable and the master out in the field most of the time, thankful to have his house run and his cows milked.

It was when she was tramping the washing one day close to the barn door that she thought to test another of Hew Phin's tricks to see the future.

That night she got the bairns abed and the mistress settled with a rug and a cog of hot milk and honey. And the master being away to Kirkwall, there was no one to spier or laugh at her, or to interrupt the little rigmarole she was going to act out. She opened both barn doors, arranged everything with care and then began to mime the winnowing of grain. Round her neck was the strap of a cubbie-basket with nothing in it except the kitchen knife pre-scribed for the magic. She threw up handful after handful of imagi-nary grain, keeping a sharp eye on the door that was open to the yard. For the story was that she should see passing the space the shadow of her future man. She gave the charade every chance . . . half-an-hour or more she tossed and watched, the only nervy moment being when she saw the master crossing the yard, home from Kirkwall. She had frozen then, with fear of discovery, but he had not seen her and, knowing that he would be cheering up his wife's quiet evening with cleck of the town's ongoings, Sara gave the winnowing a further ten minutes. Then, disgusted and planning a few tatchy words with Hew Phin about saying what was plainly not true, she hung up the cubbie and slipped back to the house.

She was just in time. The master must have gone back out again to bed his mare, while she had been closing the barn door, for there was no sign of him. But the bairns were rosy in sleep and the mistress dovering in her chair. She woke when Sara threw a peat on the fire and tucked the rug more firmly round her.

'Mester oot to rub-doon Meg, then?' she asked.

'Mester's no' hame yet, Sara. He'll maybe bide the nicht in the toon,' answered the mistress.

'But I see'd him mysel' in the yard.'

'Were y'oot in the yard? I must've been slep' then, for I didnae miss you.' Then she looked up suddenly, saw the mark of the cubbie-strap on the girl's neck and knew fine what she'd been doing out there. Sara had been restless, she minded, ever since that Gerda-one had got her bann-cries in to the minister. The mistress stared now into the fire and spoke so low and rambling that Sara heard only snatches.

'No, Sara, mester's no' hame . . .' she was silent for a moment then spoke like in a dream. . . . 'You're a guid lass tae the bairns . . . a guid lass. Mind an aye be that . . . guid tae my bairns . . .'

The master, tall, vigorous, well-favoured, young still, along-side his pale wae wife, came home in the early morning.

A month later they carried the little mistress's bier up the brae to the graveyard. The wake had been a solemn watching, for she had been no more than thirty and much loved, and there was no heart to make merry as folk often did at more timely deaths. Sara wept, and so did the sturdy widower.

But the bairns had to be fed, the peats stacked and the yard swept, life took up its rhythm again. The white-maws cried and the seasons turned above the grave on the brae. And by the time of the next Hallowe'en when Gerda was nursing the first of the pair of infants the kail-knobs had told, Sara Flett was stitching her linens to wed the master and 'be guid' to the mistress's bairns.

THE GREAT PICTISH SECRET

Those who claim to know things from the lore of their ancestors say that one of the monumental tragedies of ancient history was the loss to the people in what is now Scotland, of a very particular secret.

So deeply has it bitten into the hearts of men that the story of that grievous happening is told in different places as far apart as Eigg in the Western Isles, the Mull of Galloway and the distant north-east, where a Norwegian conqueror is said to have been one of the protagonists. All claim to be the scene of the final sad mishap. Wherever it was, something doleful happened and, give or take a detail or two, the stories told in the different places are much-of-a-muchness for likelihood, and Galloway's claim to be the origin is as good as any.

In the days of old, before Scotland was a single kingdom it was peopled mainly by the painted Picts and the Scots, two groups always at odds wherever their lands bordered on each other. Indeed they had a long-running war for dominion and eventually the Scots became the more powerful. They won battle after battle, treasure after treasure in kind and land, from the Picts, but there was one supreme prize which still eluded them and which they were determined to wrest before the struggle was done.

The prize was neither gold nor cattle stock, great weapon or precious holy relic. It was the Pictish secret of how to make the glorious drink they called their 'heather ale'. Indeed there are those who are certain sure that all the tribal warring, the skirmishing, the loss of life, were not over territory at all, but a sacrificial price to find the recipe.

If the Scots had never tasted heather ale then perhaps there would still be tribes living peacefully in their own lands. But from time to time the Scots had taken prisoners who carried small jars of the honeyed nectar strapped to their waists, and so the captors had rare tantalising sips which made them wild for more. The Picts might be a diminishing breed but they were tough, and no amount of torture or threat had made them part with word of the process by which they produced ale from heather flowers.

The Scots tried everything themselves. They infused the blossom with boiling river water, they tried crushing it in querns and mixing it with berry juice, they tried steeping it for weeks on end in dark corners, but all they achieved was bitter bree, sour water or green slime, *nothing* resembling that rich, sharp, sweet, golden liquid that warmed and ennobled them with every quaff. And so the Scots, now vastly outnumbering the Picts, conducted their campaign more vigorously than ever to batter them into submission. They almost overdid it; for folktale tellers say that, in the last great battle in the time of Kenneth MacAlpine, King of Scots, the Picts were wiped out, save for two men. These story minstrels have given several sites for that decisive conflict and it may be that there were several 'final' battles mopping up Picts in different territories. But Galloway claims the very last and that, at the end of it, only a father and son remained — as prisoners of the Scots.

Heedless, foolish Scots soldiers were ready to finish the job and rid the land forever of the plague of small red-haired men with their bow-hurdied legs and broad feet. They would surely get the ale recipe from the last generation of unprotected womenfolk. But elder statesmen and generals among the Scots, even King Kenneth himself knew better. Because the women did not have the secret of the brew. They did not rejoice in the ale as their men-folk did for it stumbled their men's legs and made them foolish and disorderly. The Scots' leaders swiftly called halt to the men who would have made a clean sweep of the Picts for with them would disappear for ever the knowledge of the heather brew.

'We will terrify them into parting with that secret,' said they. The two Picts, father and son, were brought before the victors.

'You have fought bravely,' purred one of the captains, 'and so we award you the favour of telling us how to make your heather flower wine.'

The captive son was flattered, though it was more his father's valour than his own skill that had protected him, for he was young and had fought close to the old man, protected by his whirling sword and spear. The father tightened his lips.

'There have been many spoils taken from our people in time of war, our treasures, our arms, even our womenfolk. But our heathery drink is a sacred mix, offered in time past to our gods and the life-seed dies with us.' And the boy nodded in agreement.

The Scots had several secrets of their own, one or two of them being methods of reducing, by torture, the bravest of warriors to husks of men a-quiver like aspen-grass, with terror. They named and described some of them, and man and boy turned pale. The Scots' warlords detected frissons of fear, and added several more accounts of even more highly-coloured and long-drawn-out fates of excruciating pain. It was the older man who broke down first and there was a sneering smile on the general's face as the father began to babble pitifully.

'Say . . . say no more of these fearful tortures. I . . . I'm an old man. Y . . . you would not harm an old man and if you will kill my son instead of me, without torture, I will tell you the secret.'

The general looked at him with scorn, but exultant that to him would fall the honour of discovering the ancient recipe.

'You are wise, Pict man,' he declared. 'There at yon cliff we will spare you for your son.' And the two prisoners were pushed to the nearby headland of the Mull of Galloway. There the youth was blindfolded and thrown over the brooding cliff, to the plaintive cries of guillemot and shag.

The impatient general brought his scribe to take down ingredients, process, variety of stirring-stick and pot, and whatever was the final magic incantation that would be revealed as the essence of the Pictish heather ale.

At that moment when the pen was poised and the father-warrior stood apparently shamefaced, ready to divulge the secret his race had kept from earliest times, the prisoner elbowed his guards aside and spoke . . . but not the words his enemies wanted to hear.

'My lad was young and maybe weak. He might have broken our sacred vow if he had stood alone . . . but I, never! never! never!' And with that he hurled himself over the cliff after his boy, his last shout of defiance rising up with the sea-birds he had disturbed as he fell; while the Scots stood aghast and none the wiser concerning the secret mix.

And that is why, to this day, after centuries of experiment growing the fattest ears of golden barley, brewing and blending and testing the finest malt and the purest of river water, they have never managed to match the Pictish concoction or make anything better than simple whisky, which tradition declares is a poor, poor substitute for the original heather ale.

THE PAPIST PRAYER
IN TULLIBODY KIRK

In the days of the conflict between Master Knox and Queen Mary of Scotland it was a matter of perplexity to the simple sensible peasants who farmed small stretches of land round Cambus by the River Devon, that their Christian betters were driven to such unholy ongoings in the name of religion. They themselves, some fifteen years before, had been counting their beads placidly and, apart from a few rustic hot-heads, just as placidly taken to the new religion when it was announced. Now it was 1559 and to compound the puzzle there were strange-tongued foreign soldiers stationed not so far away in Fife, under a commander by the queer name of Doysel. Folk said they were from France and were come to fight the new Kirk and try to bring back the rosary and the Holy Father; though what it was to do with Frenchmen was as much a mystery as Elizabeth of England interfering on the other side. A travelling pedlar, come to their village of late, had brought word that English ships had anchored off Fife and that troops from it were swarming ashore to fall on the Frenchies.

'Is there to be a muckle battle o' fighting over Fife way, then?' asked Hew Doak, the honest rig farmer the others looked to as their spokesman.

'The tale was that the Frenchies would be running inland this way, else there'd be slaughter, fae the big English numbers,' reported the packman.

Fighting over in Fife was one thing, but now the peasants cast fearful glances over the first shoots of their small crops, and also at the Devon, swollen with the melted snows of a hard winter just past. For the height of the water meant that the only crossing of the river was here, by the bridge they regarded as their own, because it joined the two halves of their tiny hamlet. A disorderly, retreating army and a pursuit by another one would surely spoil their winter's labour; and so they were hard put to it to care whether the Old Kirk or the New had the right of it.

But there was worse to come, for a hard-riding Englishman from the ships had reached Sir Kirkaldy Grange of the Reformers, only twenty miles away from Cambus, and even now he was sweeping a troop towards the hamlet to smash the bridge and cut off the withdrawing French. Then Kirkaldy's party was on them. Sullenly the countrymen watched them hurl destruction at their bridge and effectively slash their community in two.

'To mak' siccar there'll be a bloody tulzie as'll kill the barley and keep our meal kists tim,' said Hew gloomily.

But that mattered nothing to Sir William Kirkaldy who had his own plump stores at home, and went away again well satisfied that his allies, the English army off the ships, panting after the French papists, would cut them to pieces at Cambus, and, incidentally, revenge three dour years he himself had spent as their prisoner on Mont St. Michel.

The pounding of hooves twelve hours later told Hew and the other Cambus men that their fears were realised, and soon the dismayed Frenchmen were sliding down the steaming flanks of their horses to stare at the spating river swirling past the broken end-stumps of bridge at each bank.

The man Doysel tramped the path angrily a hundred yards upriver and downriver, then barked out strangely accented questions to a group of the crofters who were making hasty, forlorn dykes to try and protect at least a corner of their planting against the sure-coming fighting.

'More bridge?' he asked. 'Near this place?' They shrugged and shook their heads. Hew threw out both arms to convey that other crossings were miles away.

The Englishmen were not more than half a day behind them and Doysel pulled at his moustaches and spoke the Devil's name. But that was only a soldier's oath and, when he saw the old Tullibody Kirk not far off, it was God's name he said, for at heart he was a pious man and it was love of Mother Church that had brought him to this pass. Leaving his second-in-command to deploy the soldiers in a desperate last-stand formation, he walked towards the church, bared his head and went inside.

It was stripped of all that should have made it a place of worship for Doysel, no niche-statues or candles, no smile of Mary the Virgin; but it was quiet and generations of good folk had worshipped here. He knelt and asked the God of bare walls and of Holy pictures alike, to spare his men. He rose from his knees, and sat to meditate for a few moments, his weary head against the stone. Someone had come into the church behind him. It was the peasant who had spoken for the others. He sat beside Doysel, silent, then raised his hand towards the roof. Doysel looked up. His eyes took in the sturdy planking, its length and its construction and he understood that in 'asking' and 'seeking', even in this unlovely chapel, he had 'received' and 'found'.

He ran back to his men, ordered the trundling of supply carts to the church and the unloading there of ropes, pulleys and scaling ladders. Teams of soldiers slung scaffolds, hammered out the pins and wedges holding tight the hundred-year-old roof timbers, and carefully lowered them. Below, chains of men waited to swing the planks along towards the site of the smashed bridge where, after a miming parley with the commander, Hew Doak waited and watched. Then soldiers positioned the lengths of wood firmly across the river. There was an hour to spare when the waters were finally surging under the kirk roof and, rank by rank, the Frenchmen passing to the opposite bank to re-group and catch their breath in safety, further north, ready to fight another day. As the last man set foot on the far side the Cambus men looked gratefully over their undamaged rigs, and then Hew Doak beckoned them. Piece after piece of the planking was lifted and floated down to safe hiding-places under the overhang of the river's curves.

They were not the military engineers that General Doysel could command but someday, when there was peace, their church would have its roof again, over whichever of the different kind of services finally won the day. Meantime it would serve them as a moveable bridge.

In the late afternoon the English army came, seeking to slaughter the Frenchmen, who should have been penned helpless for them at Cambus. But only the fordless dark rush of the Devon confronted them and they knew they had lost their prey. Tossing horses were reined round and lately-eager men, deprived of battle, turned wearily and began the long march back to find the lea of a hill to spend the night.

The only compensation for their captains was the sight of the roofless kirk, open to the moonlit sky, which they took to have been sacked in some recent Reforming purge against the enemy Roman Church they thought of as the anti-Christ.

Sir George Maxwell, Heritor of Pollok in the 1670s, was neither the first nor the last of his family to be a kindly and benevolent laird to the people of the Pollok Shaws, the woodland village to the south of Glasgow. So it was no surprise to the loyal workers within his estate that when an outdwelling young girl, who was deaf and dumb, came into the local village looking for a work-place, the genial laird took her into service at the Big House.

Nansie Nimmo was an undersized, sallow-complexioned lass in her teen years at the time, and the years of suffering her affliction had made her ill-natured, lonely and given to startling outbursts of temper to attract attention. The first people to suffer her tantrums were the family with whom she lodged on the estate, Mistress Janet Stewart at Shaw Mill cottage, who was the widow of the former miller on the policies. She lived there with her daughter Anibel and her son John Stewart. Now they had Nansie. Nansie was truculent with the mother, jealous of the the fair-skinned Anibel's lack of handicap and her bright-faced liveliness with the lads of the Shaws. They laughed with Anibel and teased her into letting them walk with her along the banks of the White Cart River running through the estate, to steal kisses under the great chestnut trees there. When John Stewart repulsed her own clumsy efforts to attract him to the same temptations, Nansie was spiteful. She sulked and stormed inarticulately by turns and certain neighbours gossiped that Sir George's softness of heart with the incomer was hard on Janet Stewart, and that her arrival had been an ill-day for the Pollok Shaws. But none of them seriously believed that she could do real harm and were sure that she would shed her vindictiveness as she grew older.

And then the laird was taken suddenly ill.

Those who worked in the household reported that he was fevered and had stouning pains down the right side of his body.

Servants, both upstairs and down, met in knots at doorways and on the staircase, speaking of his condition in hushed tones, and they tried to take no notice of the mute maidservant who was gesticulating frantically wherever she found such groups.

At last a coachman, Rob Elder who was Kirk elder at Eastwood and in his leisure-time a righteous winkler out of sinners, understood that Nansie was declaring that there was witch-mischief afoot against the good Sir George.

'The dumb lassie has it that there's something unchancy gaun on at Widow Stewart's mill-hoose,' he explained to the others, and later to the minister. More signs from Nansie and more interpretations from the coachman.

'A doll . . . she says she seen Widow Jinty Stewart mak' a waxy doll,' he reported.

The party trooped to Shaw Mill cottage led by Nansie, who took them to the corner of the living-room. She stood on a stool and triumphantly brought down from a shelf a crudely-fashioned figure with a row of tack-pins pricked into the right side of the body. There was a hurried consultation and later a prayerful session meeting of the Eastwood elders. The minister pondered the discussion.

'There's no other course, brethren, but to ca' in the mark-finder from nearby Darnley with his witch-pin.'

He called on Mistress Stewart, and proceeded to the task of looking for such blemishes on her body as moles, strawberry stains or freckles, so that he could press in his pin to detect one that was insensible to the pain of the prick, proof that it would be the mark that the Devil had claimed her for his own.

No such mark was found on Mistress Stewart, and furthermore, three incensed neighbours said they had seen Nansie herself taking the effigy into the Stewart house. They were Bessie Weir of the next cot, Margie Craig the goatman's wife who'd been gossiping at her fence, and Margie's ancient mother who sat all day every day in the lum corner with a clay pipe, staring through the window chink, watching everyone who came or went.

So it seemed there was confusion and doubt and, in view of Sir George's speedy recovery no further steps were taken and the minister thankfully washed his hands of the matter.

For three more months Nansie glowered in her own brand of silence sulking about the Big House kitchen or in the dark corner of the cot which she had claimed as hers by planting her stool there. Then, shortly after the New Year of 1677, when Sir George was swamped again with the same fierce pains, Nansie scrambled back into the limelight. Her pinched face, mean little eyes and dramatic gestures confronted coachman and kirkmen again. She took them on a round of the estate on both sides of the river, pointing out and muttering.

'Minister,' said the coachman, 'the dumb lass has it that Widow Jinty Stewart, that's hoose you'll mind she lodges in, has been at her witchery again, and others along wi' her.'

'What others?' demanded the alarmed minister, not so adept at translating Nansie's mimes.

'John Stewart the lad, and his sister Anibel . . . aye and Bessie Weir and Mistress Craig and the old woman Jackson. She says they've all made dollies that looks like the laird . . . and pinned them for witch-spirits.'

Within the week Nansie was waving her arms about and stroking her body in sign-play to a specially-raised government commision of ministers, justiciary lords and local gentlemen. A search was made of the homes of the slandered women while Nansie smirked with satisfaction on the fringe of the appalled committee. Sure enough they found figures in all the houses, crudely formed of wax and clay, each with a cluster of pins stuck into the abdomen. No one seemed to think it strange that guilty women had not thought to dispose of such evidence when the rumours of Nansie's accusations had romped round the Shaws village and the estate.

Along with young John and his sister Anibel, all five hitherto loyal, hardworking and godly citizens were arrested and a flummoxing and terrifying interview followed, with the stern ministers, the legal word-twisting old men and the very gentry themselves. They were examined until they scarcely knew to what questions they were answering 'yea' or 'nay'. The old woman, lost without her window-chink and clay pipe, babbled in agreement that she'd given herself to Satan in her youth from 'heid to feet'; and John Stewart was persuaded to nod, that 'aye' he was 'the warlock of the Shaws'. Anibel, Widow Stewart and the neighbours also made confessions-of-sorts about their tinkering in the black arts.

There was a trial in Paisley in that year of 1677 and all were found guilty . . . victims, it was widely believed in the parish, of Nansie Nimmo's venomous charades. Having successfully caught and convicted the villains the authorities were not in the least surprised that Sir George was once again restored to his usual good health. With this signal vindication of their just handling of the matter, they had all the 'evil-doers' strangled, tarred and burned at stakes . . . all except the fourteen-year-old Anibel Stewart who, on account of her youth, was spared, but left to rot in prison.

Nevertheless, in spite of the execution of his devilish ill-wishers and to rankle the consciences of the more sensitive of the examining commission, Sir George Maxwell died the same year . . . no doubt of the simple, chronic inflammations which had ailed him all along.

A curious quirk in this tale comes to light in another history of the Maxwell family, which tells that Sir George came into the Pollok inheritance at the death of a distant kinsman. This former laird had only one child, a daughter who was deaf-mute. He therefore chose George Maxwell to be his heir. So the circumstances of Sir George's coming to his estate, and also his passing from it, were by strange co-incidence attended by the presence of deaf-dumb girls . . . unless of course, some thread in the story has strayed from the pattern and the girl at the heart of the witching was actually the disappointed heiress.

Note: The main facts of this story are true and it is told in various forms in *The Witches of Renfrewshire, Pollokshaws: Village and Burgh*, and *Satan's Invisible World Discovered*.

THE TWO MARGARETS

It's a strange thing that the arrival in the south of England in 1660 of a wordly-wise Stuart Prince to claim a crown, should have been the first link in a chain of events that led to the martyrdom of two simple women, whose quiet lives had never taken them more than a mile from their isolated hamlet, never called them beyond the Galloway hills.

Charles II with his strong dark face and his black ringlets was back in England, six foot two, even without his fancy plumed hat, and every inch a king. They say that in Edinburgh on that May day, four thousand glasses were smashed after the drinking of a welcome toast, and that as many throats roared out their joy to see the firework-scene above the castle, of Cromwell being vanquished by a vengeful Satan. Flags flew, church bells rang out, there were trumpets and drums of greeting and Mons Meg boomed out over the Nor' Loch below the rock.

The Scots had better reason than the English to be proud that day . . . . for had they not crowned Charles, King, nine years earlier, before he went into exile, and had he not declared in return for that coronation at Scone, that the church in Scotland could retain its Presbyterian ways without Prayer Book or Bishop . . . and had he not put his pen to that promise? The gloomy Cromwell was dead, life would now take up again. Long live the King!

But the rejoicing at Charles' restoration was short-lived, for either he had never had any intention of honouring that pledge, or else he had brooded over the matter as he came, more mature, to his London throne. Whatever the reason he now thought it better that church government throughout his realm should be tidied up and made uniform. But the process of tidying-up left no room for the

Presbyterian system so dearly won, a hundred years before, by the blood of the Scottish reformers . . . a system of rule by courts of equal-ranking ministers and elders.

Now Scotland growled and objected over Charles' new edicts. They remembered Jenny Geddes, the wee vegetable-seller woman, flinging her stool in St. Giles Kirk . . . and they took heart in their protests. But Charles was determined to match his northern kingdom to his English one, with the Book of Common Prayer and the setting-up of layers of clergymen there, from priests to archbishops.

The ferment of anger was slow at first but gradually it quickened and then boiled over and eventually the King made an ultimatum . . . either the Scots submitted to his will, or their pulpits and parish kirks would be taken over by more pliant men placed by patrons under the King, and their stubborn 'called' pastors expelled from their charges.

Charles had broken the first covenant and angry Scots clerics and elders drew up a second one. Several hundred ministers did not wait for Charles' response to that. They 'outed' themselves and began to organise services in quiet country moorlands, in valleys and at lochsides. All who led or attended them risked their lives.

There were running battles between worshippers and dragoons and no rebel took his stance ignorant that to be caught, and not recant the old kirk ways, was to be killed. Green tags in churchyards all over the lowlands mark the graves of men and women who died for that cause. They died on the gibbet, they died in battle and they died alone to marksmen's muskets; and that 'killing time' went on for a quarter of a century.

That was the state of affairs in the year 1684 when an outed minister in Galloway was holding field conventicles and loyal kirkfolk were bravely attending them. This tale begins with one such service, taking place on a Sabbath morning near the little town of Wigtown, on the Bladnoch river estuary. The congregation met in a grassy hollow, starred that day with spring wildflowers.

A dipper-bird swooped from boulder to boulder along the river, the last Psalm had risen on the wind and the minister spoken a benediction, when a look-out rode down on a steaming horse to tell them that the dragoons were on their way. Like ghosts the gathering melted away separately as they had learned to do, some by riverside paths, others along the nearby shore or into hidden ways between low hills and hummocks. The minister was led hastily to a nearby cot where he was quickly dressed in the gudeman's clothes, against the chance of a search being made.

It was all a fine brave adventure for the young and fleet. But it was harder for the older folk, who were halt or breathless, to get to hiding. That morning most got safe away, but there was a group of women making slower progress, who were spotted and rounded up at gunpoint by red-coats under the command of a young officer determined on showing, not only his authority, but his fitness for promotion.

Three of that plodding group, had they deserted the fourth, could have run off as lightly as the rest, but they had with them Margaret Lachlan, over sixty years old and ailing.

Charles II himself had recently died leaving not only his kingdom to his brother James but his wayward stubborn principles as well. The authorities in Scotland were now thoroughly alarmed. They were battling with the unabated crusading fervour of the rebellion, its long-drawn-out course continuing into this turbulent new reign, and with the fanatical fury of some of the Covenanters themselves. In the panic, courts and hearings were hasty and ill-conducted and even the smallest suspicion of being a sympathiser brought down establishment wrath. As in many another place, local conformers and army men were appointed accusers, judges and jurors and in the mockery of a trial that these four women stood, they faced four neighbour-men and a major of the dragoons, John Winram.

Margaret Lachlan, now in her declining years, waited for her sentence one May day, along with Margaret Wilson, who was eighteen; her small sister Agnes, still but a child; and a terrified maidservant Daisy Maxwell. The court considered itself lenient, since Daisy was merely attending on the others, in sentencing her only to be flogged through the streets and wynds of Wigtown from court-room to home. And it thought the thirteen-year-old Agnes lucky that her father Gilbert Wilson was able to ransom her back for a hundred pounds. The father was stricken for his older girl and her elderly companion, but both of them were reckoned to be fine well-aware of what they were doing and of age to pay the penalty. The penalty was death. But by no instant bullet or quick gibbeting.

The judges and the soldiery were to act executioners too, and under the fine Major Winram they escorted the two Margarets roughly towards the shore. There, at low tide when the estuary of the Bladnoch was no more than bleak mud flats, two stakes had been driven into the river bed. One stake was a yard or two further out than the other and the older Margaret was lashed to it while Margaret Wilson was tied to the other.

The Solway tide has ever been a slow, sliding lid of water. The women would watch it creeping in, bringing death slowly, and it was hoped and expected that when the younger one saw Margaret Lachlan overcome and drowned dead, she herself would convert quickly to King, Bishop, Prayer Book and foisted minister.

The tide lapped first at Mistress Lachlan's feet and then at Margaret Wilson's . . . in half an hour it was at their knees and, as the day wore on, at their thighs, waists then breasts. With a shudder and a pitiful gasping for breath Margaret Lachlan's body drooped dead on the stake . . . and the water eased up to Margaret Wilson's neck.

'Margaret Wilson, you're young. If you but pray for the King, you'll live,' urged Rab Grierson, one of the neighbours.

'I'll pray for the King only that he repent his harm to God's kirk.' And she lifted her chin and began to sing the Shepherd's Psalm.

'Tak' your oath to the King's command!' ordered a tall soldier whose duty that day was to be out at the stakes, himself in the rising water.

'No sinful oaths from me!' she insisted.

'Tak' the oath, Meg Wilson,' pleaded the crowd of onlookers. The soldier was impatient now and ducked her head once, to let her taste her fate.

'Tak' the oath, lassie!'

'Never! I am one of Christ's children. Let me go to Him.'

'Tak' another drink then, hinny.' And he thrust her head under the water and held it there until Margaret Wilson too, slackened, and slumped on the stake. Then to a low moan from the crowd and a few brave jeers the soldier waded ashore and shook himself like a dog, while the whaups cried a dirge over the estuary and the fields beyond.

There are those who claim that a reprieve was on its way to Wigtown that day. But that is ever the story of shame-faced folk who bring about a martyrdom. Excuses are of no moment, the fact remains that the two godly women lie under a kirkyard monument still remembered three hundred years on. And the Martyrs' stake (a solid cairn now on that bleak estuary) marks the place where the Margarets were drowned to death for their three sins . . . for praising their Lord outdoors in the midst of his creation . . . for defying first King Charles whose broken pledge had wrought havoc in his northern kingdom . . . and for denying allegiance also to his brother. But King James was even less of a diplomat in religious matters than Charles. He was mistrusted in England as well as Scotland and, even as the two were dying, his own days as monarch were numbered.

SPUNK KATE'S MONOPOLY

In the Glasgow of the 1830s there was a kind of demi-monde of street characters who lived by their wits and even made their disabilities work for them. In that world of survival by wile and guile, moved the woman they called Spunk Kate. That was her style in the summer when she sold trinkets, tape and crude matches. In winter she was Kate the Creel and sold herrings round the town. She did have a wedge of a room in the Briggait, off Salt-market, a little dark place in a building that had been added as an afterthought to an ancient gable wall, but she spent much of her time in the streets with her wares, going round the better houses edging the Green and even tramping out to the Langside village to the south. She was plump and glowing as a rose-hip, from her diet of herrings and oatmeal and from taking the river winds on her skin as she padded back and forth across the old Clyde bridge.

Indeed Kate was quite well-put-on among her circle of half-vagrant friends . . . a Glasgow group of the time who supported and defended each other when any of them came into conflict with authority. There was Rab Hall who could consume pies by the half dozen, setting his appetite against wagers. There was Hawkie the chapman, and there were Mary the Cloggie-dancer and her crippled partner, the street singer they called 'the Major'. Among them all Kate with her bright eyes and sonsy curves was a goodly, cheerful sight.

She made a sparse living in winter, buying herrings cheap at the Broomielaw (a day old and not quite fresh) and selling them nevertheless as 'caller herring'. Her summer living was even poorer when she carried her packtray with knick-knacks on it that brought her no more than a few pence a day.

That was the state of Kate's livelihood when she first met up with a pair of tinks when she was over south of the river, Kingston way, one autumn day.

She was refreshing herself in an ale-cot there and exchanging clash with a couple on a bench by the door. The tink woman had her teeth clenched on a clay pipe and when she made to light it she took out a paper fold of match sticks and rasped one on the stone cot wall.

Now Kate was ever one with an eye to the possibilities of what she saw. Old-type Congreve and Promethean matches that needed little bottles of asbestos and sulphuric to set them alight were part of her stock-in-trade (as of every other pedlar's), but this was something new . . . this producing the tiny flare with no more than a scart on the wall. But Kate was canny. She picked up the spent match.

'Your clay's fair drawin' . . . tak's a good licht to set it up like that,' she said casually.

'Aye, it's a braw thing the Deil's stick,' said the woman. The man spat expertly at a stone.

'Seen them first doon Ayr way,' said the woman. 'They dips the spunky in a paste of pottish and monk's poison and dries it, that way it sparks on a wall or a bit iron. . . . There y'are, tak' yin yoursel'.'

Kate took it, changed the chat to other things and slipped it into her shawl pocket.

'Are you for the toon?' she asked, ready to invent an outbreak of the plague there, to warn them off what might be her market for the new match.

'Na, na, we dinna never gang over the river. There's law men in the toon as chases tinks.' The man put down his ale-jar and jerked his head at the woman, then Kate watched them trundle their hand-cart on to the road that led towards Paisley.

Thoughtfully she made her own way home across the south-side meadow, gathering up twigs and scraps of wood as she went. The pickings, though, were few, for others before her had been collecting firewood for the night.

'Pottish, monk's poison and a wee tate gum to mak' a paste,' the tink had said. Kate called at the drysalter, before turning into the Briggait.

There was a perfect fury of chamfering, dipping and drying spunks of wood, into what the tinks had called 'Deil's sticks' and three days later Kate's new product hit the streets of Glasgow. The first Lucifers.

In six weeks she was doing a thriving wee trade, taking her matches round the grand houses where she sold her fish, and over the river-bridge into the meadow villages.

It was one late afternoon when she was walking home with her baskets that she first met Rab the carter. He ambled his nag alongside her and touched a great Kilmarnock bonnet.

'Am I richt for the Glasgow bridge, mistress?'

'Aye so. Just the way you're goin'.'

'Put your gear in the cart and I'll gie you a ride,' he offered. She threw on her baskets and clambered up beside him, he flicked a rein and on they jogged.

'What are you lookin' for in the toon?'

'My fortune.'

She looked at him and thought privately he wouldn't find it in his face, but he was a pawky enough wee chap, and she enjoyed his company fine for the short ride.

Kate had often thought to take a mate, but until now she had been too canny a body ever to have put herself in the hands of just any Tom or Harry. But of late, with her brisk business, she had been feeling that she had a modest competence to keep her independence even in marriage. She was past the age to be thirled with bairns and could go on with her pottish and gum spunks, wed or no.

She saw Rab the Carter a time or two more. He made her laugh each time and, in spite of his short size, and bow hurdies, she decided to wed him. Old lore doesn't say whether he hummed or hawed when she told him, but it's likely he jumped at the chance for, as Mary the cloggie-dancer said to the Major when she heard of the match. . . . 'Fancy him landin' the likes o' Kate Spunk!'

Rab moved himself into the Briggait room and his horse to the courtyard stall in the back alley. Like many a wee man who marries above himself, Rab was no sooner wed than he was laying down the law to his gude-wife and, for all they were the flotsam of the city, to Rab's mind there were lower.

'Mind you and no' tagle and clash wi' them tinks out the King's town when you're ower at the big hooses.'

But Kate was not for browbeating. She had not met the pottish-and-gum tinks again but there were others she'd always bought trish-trash off for her tray, when they took their ale together.

'When you sets me up in ribbons and silks, Rab Carter, you'll can bid me this and that. Afore then, just get your cairt awa' and do a bit cadging yoursel' if you're to sup the nicht.'

The good days lasted a week or two more, and then as summer folded by, and winter was on them hard, folk were needing fires, and wood was hard to come by for the spunks. There wasn't so much making on the fish, for they'd to be bought, and anyway there was cholera in the town and folk had a dour suspicion of fish. It was a cold trade too. The matches made an easier living. . . . If they could find the wood there would be no limit to sales.

Rab's carting trade was low too now, for two smart youths along the Trongate had set up in business with two spanking new painted carts and glossy high-stepping ponies to match them.

Kate and Rab did not sink into despair but they began to row.

'Ca' yersel' a man . . .' began Kate. He never had . . . and in fact had been much surprised to find himself one, after they were wed. 'If you cannae get cadgin' find siller some ither way.'

He bristled.

'An' you Mistress. Are you goin' to find some way forbye herrin', for you'll no' find wood for your spunkies?'

'Aye, I'll find wood for my spunkies, a'richt,' Kate assured him hotly.

'An' so'll I get siller,' retorted Rab, slapping his bonnet on his grey head and clattering out into the dark of the Briggait night.

Kate sat on, wondering at her rash vow. No use to search for wood that night for it was moonless dark. Tomorrow she would scour the riverbank . . . even out Carmyle way if needs be. She'd go tramping the most of the day, but first she'd see the Major and Mary buried at the Ramshorn, for the two, sangster and dancer, had been taken with the cholera a week since, and died only a day apart.

Rab was out all night, though three times Kate heard him at his cart down the back. At daybreak he threw himself on the chaff in the corner.

'Beat wi' sleep,' he muttered, then told her he'd been round every stable in the town removing horse-shoes that he'd sell to the smith over Gorbals way when he'd had an hour's rest. 'I'll awa' afore the hue an' cry's up and folk starts lookin' for them.'

Kate agreed he'd done quite well. She herself washed her face for the funeral, saw off Mary and the Major in the Ramshorn Kirk-yard, and then set out with her basket. She jinked into a garden or two of the city mansions, but they were kept clear of twigs and branches. There was a box outside a provision grocer's but as she reached it, his hand shot out and whisked it inside and she had to content herself with an orange that fell out of the box as he lifted it.

She passed the town hospital where Mary and the Major had died and spared a thought for the pair lying decently-kisted in the Ramshorn. 'Decently-kisted' . . . that was because their landlady had had a line from the hospital 'ceptor to get kists off the mort-room carpenter. Glasgow magistrates had a worthy taste to see their vagrants off respectably. Kate's walk quickened. She turned back, went down past the Briggait room; threw in her basket and set off at a trot across the river bridge.

Would any of them be there . . . the tinks that Rab had such a gringe at?

The Town Hospital Preceptor sat at his desk having his withers wrung near to tears by the broken tinker-man who stood before him trembling with grief. The cholera wasn't just in the city, it seemed. It had reached across to the south bank of the Clyde and beyond. And at that very moment the man's wife and two of his children lay dead over there, in a broken-down herd-cot, waiting for burial.

'My Nancy'll no rest easy gin I dinna tak' her oot Kilbarchan way for the burial. I have my push-cart and my other bairns to take a hand w'it. But gin Your Lordship could someways see me right for simple kists, it would put the thing the way it should be for Nancy and the bairns.'

Even if the Preceptor had not also quite liked the 'Lordship', he interpreted his duties humanely and sent the stricken widower off with chitties to the hospital carpenter for one large and two small coffins, which would be delivered by a boy in the late afternoon down the Briggait, where the tink would be waiting in the street for them outside a friend's house.

The Preceptor could scarcely do the round of his morning duties for thinking on the plight of the itinerant (with such a right respect for authority) shorn suddenly of wife and bairns, and left to manage the rest of his family. The official was a godly man and when his day's work was done, and before he went home to his sup, he made his way down the Saltmarket to the door-number in the Briggait that the man had given him, to see that he had received the kists. In his pocket was a small purse of money to ease the fellow's way for a day or two.

As he reached the place, he could hear a waft of unseemly merriment from the window chink above, and a great hammering and splintering of wood. Curiously he went upstairs and pushed open a half-hinged door on a scene it took him years to forget. Kate and the Tink and Rab the Carter sat about the room, the cadger with a growing pile beside him of spunk sticks he was chiselling out of a mort-kist, Kate dipping and turning their tips in an acrid-smelling paste and laying them in rows to dry; while the Tink replenished jars of ale as fast as they were emptied.

The three fell sheepishly silent and the Preceptor looked round the room with its weeping walls, rickety table and two chairs without backs. A chaff bed lay in a corner with a tattered rug thrown across it and there was neither dish nor ornament to be seen. The large coffin and one of the small ones were still intact. He could repossess them, but there was no way he could recoup from this lot, the loss of the third. Besides he was in his job precisely because he knew how many beans made five, and realised that the already smashed kist would provide Kate with enough matches and profit to keep her and her man out of trouble for a long time to come.

As for the tinker; the town jail was too full of more violent felons to leave room for a vagrant who would find its shelter no punishment anyway.

'Be off wi' you, tink. Think lucky you're no' for a cell, and dinnae let's see your face in this toon again.'

No one did badly out of the matter. The two whole kists went to more deserving cases and the Preceptor's kindly purse, intended for the poor widower's comfort would go some way to pay the third. The tink went off with his share of the matches and with the new-found talent for melodrama which in times-coming he offered occasionally to strolling players he met in his travels, Kate and Rab had the spunks, and the assurance that the secret of their making would remain safely out of town.

Spunk Kate had her monopoly as long as she needed it. The magic of her matches became a by-word and brought folk to seek her out. And when the Preceptor, on his way around the town, saw her doing a brisk trade, he couldn't help having a wee chuckle to himself. So maybe that was a bonus for him. But he never told the tale to the carpenter.

The kirk in the parish of Durness was a poor shell of a place, an ancient chapel built far back beyond the memories of any who still attended it, or even any of their grandsires. Some said it was there in the time of the great Crusades. Weighted ropes held down the thatch against the toss of an ill-wind from the North-Atlantic; even so it hung tangled over slit windows which scarcely let in a shaft of sunlight. The low walls were of uneven boulders cobbled together with daub dry enough on the outside with sun and wind, but inside cold and sweating. If it had ever been built to the glory of God there was precious little glory about it now. And yet week by week the faithful made their way to attend its services and listen to its worthy minister . . . from the crofters and fisherfolk, to the dominie and Lord Reay of the big house, himself.

In the days when, as a lad, he had sat on the Laird's bench in that kirk, with his back against the wetness of the wall, he had wished that his father would give the people a new kirk, dry, light and sturdy against storm to make their Sabbaths fine for them. At that time he thought his father a penny-pinch for never having built such a place but now, as Laird himself, he had discovered that a man might inherit a stretch of land and a solid residence, but that with a tenantry who could barely survive off their tiny, gravelly, cliff-top patches, there was no great income to his estate, beyond their meagre renderings to him of kain and labour.

As Reay tramped throughout the turn of the seasons along the white curve of Balnakiel shore, he would look up at the crumbling kirk far above him and brood. And many a Sabbath after worship he walked round and round the outside of the kirk measuring it stride by stride and studying to see how much of the old structure was sound enough to make a foundation for a restored building. At home he counted and re-counted what assets of the Reay family could be turned to stone and wages and the sum total always fell pitifully short. The matter began to obsess him, day and night, but there seemed to be no answer as to how he could provide a decent kirk for his people and their God. Most serious of all it filled his mind in the time of preaching to the exclusion of most of what the minister was saying.

Maybe that was why he fell finally to what his people (had they known of it) might have called an accommodation with the devil.

Now there was another man in the parish with a teasing problem, one Donal MacMurchov. His worry was not poverty. Indeed he had a greater share than most of his fellows, of the world's paltry goods of the early 1600s. For Donal was a secret highwayman as well as a crofter, and although his night-riding territory was not very widespread it provided him with an extra meal of cheese or ale from those who carried such supplies on journeys in and out of the parish; or he sometimes took a shilling or two where he judged his victim well-enough-off not to miss them. He was selective in his molesting, and unviolent. He never intended physical harm, and anyway the ancient pistol he brandished was stiff with rust. Another little source of pence for Donal was one which fed on the superstition of fishermen along the coast, that they could buy fair winds from the masked 'stranger' when he stopped them on misty early mornings on their way down to their boats.

Their highwayman was no real danger to the people of Balnakiel, but Lord Reay himself felt that having such a man at large besmirched the good name of his lands. Like other local folk he had a fair suspicion that MacMurchov's stony little croft, some two hundred yards from his nearest neighbour the parish mason, did not supply the living Donal enjoyed. But no one had ever caught and unmasked the man. Nights were dark on that wild coast and the half-blind old nag that took Donal to his favourite ambush corners and might have been recognised, was generally tethered out of sight when the highwayman made his catch.

But Donal, however devil-may-care his calling, had moments of terror that had to do only indirectly with his wild night-riding. He might be a wicked, sinning highway-robber, but he *had* learned what was what at his mother's knee, and his one dread in life was that, when he made an end of it, he would not be allowed to lie at peace in hallowed ground. This fear had come too late for him to mend his ways, for the harm was done and he had a list of crimes to his discredit as long as all the tombstone legends put together that were already in the kirkyard . . . the very kirkyard where he longed to be laid to rest when that melancholy day arrived. The Balnakiel and Durness folk might not be solemn certain that their highwayman was MacMurchov, but they would be sure enough of it to bury him when the time came, outside the graveyard with the suicides, the unwed mothers and the bastard bairns. The matter preyed sore on Donal's mind, but when a night for riding came, the excitement would creep over him and he would have to go.

His routine was habit with him now, scratching or hoeing at his poor soil by day and watching for the sky signs that foretold a moonless night: then he would don black face-scarf and dark plaid, stick the pistol in his belt, throw a fold of blanket over his nag's back, hobble off past the cave of Smoo on the track down Loch Eribollside, to wait for a lonely unwary traveller.

Now it happened that the night of the very day when Donal counted he was having his fortieth birthday was velvet black and perfect for a foray and he set out as usual on the old horse. Loch Eriboll lay there, deep, still and invisible, somewhere out beyond the track. At this milestone in his life he was pre-occupied as he rode, turning over thoughts of the ultimate fate of his immortal soul, and so perhaps he was uncharacteristically careless.

Normally, even in such darkness, even before he was close enough to see a man's face, he knew something of a rider or walking traveller. He could tell whether he was light or heavy, lean or stout, he knew whether a man was in haste or at leisure from the urgency of hoof or step, and by the tap of a staff or a voice to a horse whether old or young. He could tell too whether a mount was a fine one or, like his own, an ambling cuddy. His usual alertness to all of these signs should have told him now that the man rounding the bend towards him, was tall and well-made, not weary but lively in the saddle, and no older than himself. He should have detected that he was riding a good horse at a brisk pace and that the form and figure was as familiar to him as the minister's own would have been . . . the kind of traveller best left alone to proceed unhindered on his way.

But Donal's thoughts that night were awry. He was too hasty with his pistol across his wrist and when the rider was still twenty yards away he barked out his usual command, 'Halt ye, traveller, or I fire!'

In reply the tall rider urged on his horse and, as he came close, leapt from his saddle on to Donal tumbling him to the ground and not only enveloping him in his great plaid but gathering him in a pair of arms as tight as the gird of a barrel. The pistol went flying harmlessly out of reach, the two rolled and grappled on the ground, grunting and soughing, now one on top, now the other until finally the brave highwayman was on his back, with the victim, who should have been begging for mercy, astride him, pulling loose his face kerchief and letting it lie askew around his neck. Both pairs of eyes were well able at this close range to recognise what they saw, but the robber's were more shocked than the traveller's.

'Lord Reay, sir!' stammered Donal.

'Indeed, indeed it is, MacMurchov,' agreed the Laird. Donal groaned, uncovered at last, his mind awhirl with thoughts of unblessed bairns, self-killers and witches, all damned like himself to wander as lost souls, outcasts for ever from holy kirkyards.

Lord Reay saw the abandoned pistol and, swinging himself off Donal, picked it up and sat with his back against a tree, levelling it now at the highwayman. Donal sat up and took off his scarf, looking all the while along the gunbarrel.

'It doesna work,' he confessed.

'I see that. But it could put a terror in folk all the same.'

'Aye, Laird, you're right there,' admitted Donal. 'I canna peace the fears of my conscience just by knowing it wouldna kill.'

'Your conscience . . . your fears! What fears does a highway-thief have?' Lord Reay put down the gun, took a pinch of snuff and offered the box to Donal. It all seemed quite companionable there in the dark.

'Oh aye, I have my fears, Laird . . . it's been my bad dread this long while back, that when the good Lord takes me to death the minister and elders'll no' put me to lie in the kirkyard.' Lord Reay picked up the pistol again and swung it thoughtfully by the trigger-guard.

'You're not an old man yet, MacMurchov. By the time you're ready for your mort-kist, the kirk itself'll likely be crumbled to dust, for it's in a poor way now, a poor, poor way.'

There was silence for a few moments, each man lost gloomily in his own regrets.

Then the Laird spoke with sudden new interest in his voice.

'I suppose there's no great takings can be made this way?' he asked, tapping the gun with a long aristocratic finger. Donal babbled his anxiety to make as little as possible of his infamies.

'Not with my old mare there, for a mile or two's as far as she goes, easy. And it's not that many passers-by comes near here. You can see for yourself too, that I havenae a very fierce weapon.'

'You could go further with a fleeter horse then . . . and do better with a good pair of firearms?'

Donal felt like a fish on a hook. What trick was this the Laird was playing to fankle him?

'The fast horse, aye. Fine pistols would match it . . . but I wouldnae kill or even hurt, and that's the truth.'

'But you could fire in the air . . . would that not empty a few purses . . .?'

It was a queer thing (if any but the two had known of it) that a road-robber and a fine milord should have found enough to keep them talking together there at the lochside, until near dawn. . . .

In the next few days there was clash among the Balnakiel, Durness and Eriboll folk, that their Laird, on that black night had got the better of the robber who had brought a bad name to the district and had unmasked a face that was quite strange to these parts. It was said that he had sent the villain packing far away, off to wherever he came from. Minding their own past suspicions of Donal MacMurchov they began greeting him with a new, shame-faced warmth.

They never again heard of an ambush within fifteen miles of the parish, but there were tales from further afield beyond Eriboll, Tongue and Hope, and even furth of Scourie, of some new wild highwayman flourishing gleaming pistols, firing them threateningly into the air, emptying purses of gold coin from rich travellers, and lightening ladies in carriages of their fancy necklaces and rings. And then, they said, he would fly off through the night on a huge black Arab mare not unlike the one Lord Reay himself had lately sold somewhere in the south. Although it was never told that anyone had suffered hurt, mothers scolded bairns into fear of him and grand folk began to travel in parties.

Of Lord Reay's encounter with Durness's own night-thief, it seemed to his tenantry that the good God rewarded his courage in tackling the man for, after it, his fortunes took a turn for the better . . . so fine a turn in fact, that within a few years the people were thanking him that the minister was preaching in a trig-built little kirk that was the envy of many another parish. It was raised on the same spot where the old one had stood above the white rim of the shore, and it bore the date A.D. 1619.

Donal MacMurchov was a diligent worshipper there and when, in the ripeness of years, he passed to his reward, he was buried with all respect at the south wall of the new kirk.

If his neighbour, the stone mason who carved a skull and cross-bones at his head, knew any more than any of his fellows he wisely kept it to himself. After all, many a worthy man's stone had that old symbol for decoration. He kept it to himself at least until it did not matter to either Donal or Laird Reay that MacMurchov had been seen slipping out of his cottage of a dark night and making for the Laird's stable . . . and that the next day north Sutherland was agog with the latest exploits of the highwayman on the black mare.

And whether, afterwards, Donal MacMurchov lay any easier in his six feet of consecrated ground than Lord Reay himself in his, is not for the likes of story-tellers or their readers to speculate.

However tragic the end of the Forty-Five rebellion at Culloden moor, men have sung with pride in the years since then of the honour that was salvaged by the loyalty of men and women all over Scotland to the Prince they would not sell for a fortune of thirty-thousand pounds. So tiny was the number of those who deliberately failed him or his cause, that they have been, ever since, the more despised.

Margaret Ferguson, new-wed wife, glanced shyly at her husband as they stood before the minister for his final homily. The shyness was but for the occasion and her new married state, for she was naturally a lively girl, winsome and vivacious, delighting in life . . . as much in her fearless riding across the countryside as in her light-foot dancing at great house-parties and assembly-room balls. She was young, some might have said 'giddy' and, before now had given little thought to the ills or just causes of the world. Not like the grave, intelligent, young lord beside her. She sighed, ever so slightly, wondering if she would ever match up to him.

John Murray of Broughton was Border-born, son of a much respected and noble house. He was not above middle height but he had bearing, presence and a proud light in his eye — the good looks of his forebears that were more attractive than mere height.

Like many high-born young Scots, John Murray had been educated in Edinburgh and then abroad in Leyden and in Rome. There the Scots expatriate and student circle lived and moved and entertained itself around the little court held by the man they called James VIII of Scotland and III of Great Britain. The older exiles consorted, sympathised and plotted with James, while the young ones, like Johnnie Murray, gathered round his mercurial and fascinating son, Charles Edward Stuart.

Another father than Sir David Murray might have wondered

how much studying was being pursued in Rome by his son, but Sir David had fought for James the Chevalier in 1715, and thought it quite proper that his son should cleave to the Bonnie Prince. The prospect of restoring the Stuarts to their heritage seemed not only exciting to John but entirely right and just. He was a valuable blend for such an adventure, daring, romantic, yet methodical and painstaking. During those years in Rome he became indispensable to Charles who called him his Secretary. Little by little the two men, with others in their group, established a network of support, cast from Rome to Paris, London to Edinburgh and the North.

A first invasion attempt was to be made in the south of England when the time was right, and it was the great hope that mile by mile the country would fall to Charles . . . that it was waiting to be taken like ripe fruit. To this end John Murray came back to Scotland in 1738, to manage his estates certainly, but dedicated to preparing there for the uprising against the Hanovers. It was during this time that the earnest John met and married his lovely Margaret.

If the new mistress at Broughton had never previously bothered her pretty head about anything more than her pleasures, and the domestic tasks and accomplishments necessary to the smooth and seemly running of a laird's household, she was nevertheless intelligent and her husband's absorption with his cause soon began to intrigue her.

There was much to do . . . a word here, the copying of a secret letter there, the counting of men, the making of maps and charts, tallies of arms and ammunition, lists of sympathisers and opponents. Margaret, willy-nilly, became immersed in the documenting and checking of information and the careful locking away of it all every night, into a stout casket.

And there was the new task she had set herself for, day by day, evening by evening, she and her maids were folding and stitching white silk into bonnet cockades for the Prince's army, and the pile of them in the log baskets beside the fireplace was growing.

Time and again in those waiting years Johnny spoke of Charles Edward in glowing terms, of the tall, lean, athletic and strikingly handsome figure. . . .

'Every inch a King . . . and book-learned, Meg . . . no' like yon wee stout German there, that looks no more likely than a lazy gate-porter.'

Margaret would nod and snip the thread of yet another cockade and drop it into the basket. She tried to visualise such a Prince and enter into John's enthusiasm for the raising of his standard and the march of his men across the land. And yet, behind all her support with the letter-writing, sewing and lists there was a persistent niggle of practical common sense that made her wonder a little at the wisdom of upsetting the comparative peace and stability that was abroad in the land under the 'lazy gate-porter', whose only crime was to lack the royal charisma of the Stuarts.

But she stifled that thought that was so disloyal to John, and remembered that he was clever and serious and must know better than she, what was best for the country.

1742, '43, '44, the years turned on, the plans matured and the Catholic King of France was behind them. But at the same time government opposition to the Stuart supporters was growing. A whisper that a man was a Jacobite brought questioning and arrest, confiscation of land, or worse. Secretary Murray was in Edinburgh for much of his time, controlling, directing, disseminating information. But there were loose tongues about his activities now and the authorities waited only for some scrap of real evidence to convict him.

In this haar of rising suspicion he brooded over those caskets of documents at Broughton that would bring death or ruin to those whose names were listed there. And he thought of the great baskets of white cockades. A message and the strongbox key were smuggled to a neighbouring laird there in Peeblesshire, in the spring of 1744; the cockades went down into dark cellars and the casket was carried to the neighbour's kitchen garden and buried there. By the early summer kail was growing above it as if the ground had never been disturbed.

And while he worked ceaselessly for the cause, still Margaret brooded on the wisdom or the folly of bloodshed to come.

The story does not tell when Lady Margaret first laid eyes on

Charles Edward Stuart. Perhaps she was with her husband when he went to meet the Prince, arriving at last in July 1745 at Eriskay, set on restoring the crown to his father. Whenever that first sighting was, of the handsome figure with the crusading light in his eyes, Margaret Murray of Broughton was his devoted disciple from that moment, convinced beyond doubt that this man would, in the future, be her rightful King.

As he gathered support and won his way mile after mile from the west, John Murray smoothed his path, ever at his elbow, an able organizer and administrator. Alongside them Mistress Margaret rode her mare hard from place to place, weaving and curling round the countryside, offering a hand to kiss, and one of her white cockades, to every recruit she won for her Prince.

Then for a time her duties took her away from the army, to go ahead of it and gather support, and she and John saw little of each other. But then there came a glorious September day in Edinburgh when, to the skirling of pipes, fifes and drums and celebratory musket shots in the air, to the clatter of hooves under mounted clansmen, Charles Edward, in tartan coat and blue bonnet, had his father declared King James III and himself Prince Regent. On that day John and Margaret Murray sat their horses, side by side, excited, proud, and more in love than at any time since their marriage. It was a high moment both of them remembered for the rest of their lives. Then John moved forward to direct the Prince through the crowds, while Margaret, erect and happy in the saddle, held up a drawn sword in salute and then offered to those who drew theirs for Charles, her hand and her cockade.

The old grey walls of Edinburgh echoed to the celebration revelry, with one common sigh the gentlefolk daughters of the city lost their hearts to the Prince, while their brothers pressed forward eagerly, and their fathers raised canny bonnets, excited enough, but minding themselves not to get carried away, lest the rebellion was but a flash in the pan that could leave them ruined.

Then in a short time John Murray was off south with the Prince, and Margaret, certain of a victorious outcome to all their plans, went home to Broughton, to wait her next call to duty.

Maybe that guarded cheer from the sires of Edinburgh, that shadow of doubt, was a straw in the wind. For the Jacobite army marched south finding less support as it went. The folk in the north of England might sentimentally toast the King-over-the-water across their fancy goblets but, beyond Manchester, they kept their swords in their sheaths. Hearts round Prince Charles Edward began to falter. And although by the time they reached Derby, there was consternation in London at their advance, the first real doubts and dissensions began in the Prince's army. These became more insistent and, when there was no word of reinforcements, two to one among its leaders declared that it was time to turn back.

The retreat straggled north and into Scotland. Margaret Murray joined them as they trudged, to offer her cockades again, her hopes never wavering. But few wanted her badges now and those who had taken them so gallantly a few short months before, began to peel off the main troop as it went, slipping home to see to their rigs and their families and promising to come back if prospects for the Prince improved.

It was Margaret now who was having to raise her husband's flagging spirits, for he was exhausted and ill. And when the remaining clansmen lined up at Culloden for their last brave stand against King George II's well-drilled men who had by-passed them on the march, Murray of Broughton lay at his lodging in Elgin while his fellow rebels were being slaughtered thirty miles away.

The cruel aftermath of that bloody battle is part of this story only so far as it concerns John and Margaret Murray. Barely recovered, Broughton, in one final frantic effort, crossed and re-crossed the countryside by mountain and glen, promising that there were troops and trunks of gold for pay and supplies on their way from France. But the Highlanders had lost heart and by the time the French gold arrived, most ordinary clansmen were dispersed and, among the rest there was doubt and suspicion about the distribution by their leaders of the Louis d'or.

No one had ever doubted Murray of Broughton's honour before, but now, when the money was taken to Lochaber to be kept safe until the rebellion revived, there were whispers that he was hoarding it against his own future. That it disappeared at that time and was never recovered, keeps a second shadow hanging over Murray's name.

The much greater shadow though, is cast by a bigger, blacker cloud. Whether his ill-health and the accusations against him by men whose respect he counted on, turned his loyalty sour, who can say? He lost heart and from being a rallying hero for his Prince, he became a fugitive. But unlike the hardy royal wanderer, who never lost his charm or humour, Murray skulked from place to place, haggard, grey and tattered. And while Charles clowned with brave good spirits as Betty Burke, and companionably ate dry bread with others in caves, Broughton, miserable and alone, posed as a travelling herd.

Even a sad last meeting at Loch Sunart with his brave Margaret, who was herself trying to elude the dragoons, did not mend his bruised spirit . . . served rather to burden it further . . . for Margaret, wandering like a gipsy, was eight months pregnant and uncomfortable with his child. But unlike him, she remained optimistic and still concerned for her Bonnie Prince.

It was at home, only a mile from his house at Broughton, that King George's dragoons finally ran Murray to earth. He had no stomach now for the fight or even the compensation of going down in history as a martyr. The casket of lists might be mouldering away under the kail in the Border country, but Government lawyers had no need of them now. In exchange for the saving of his own life and for his ultimate freedom, Broughton spilled out the names they wanted, group by group, one of them, that of his own friend Lord Lovat, who, on Murray's evidence, went to the block.

Meantime Margaret spent a hard month, hunted from cot to cot, reaching her mother in Edinburgh at last, and then hurried from one hiding place to the next there. An offer to tell all she knew would surely have allowed mercy to a woman so near childbirth. But that was not for the Lady of the White Cockade. In a cold attic south of Edinburgh she bore a son whom she defiantly named Charles. He survived only a few hours and her sorrow was compounded by hearing that her husband was a prisoner in London. Sadly Margaret packed her bags, found her own way south and took back-street lodging with a milliner, near to where he was held.

It was then that reports of John's craven behaviour began to reach her. Jacobite callers with little understanding or reticence were not slow to tell her that her husband had lost all respect and that as day succeeded day he was the more reviled. Some stopped calling on her altogether, visiting his shame on her. She, herself, began to see him as two different men . . . the strong, loyal secretary who held his trust to the Prince almost sacred; and the ailing coward who had betrayed his friends. And her heart ached for both of them.

She might have remained in London but, although her husband had secured his own neck, there was no word yet of his release. If he was given his freedom there would surely be no place for him either here in London, or among neighbours in Peeblesshire who despised him. Margaret was still heart-loyal to both husband and Prince and a sudden hope surged in her that this might be all a ruse on John's part for the greater good of the Stuarts . . . that he would be freed eventually and join the Prince in Rome, living to fight another day. And so Margaret Murray was persuaded to slip out to a small ship that would take her to the continent to prepare a home for him. Some who saw her go said later that she was as proud as ever as she stood on deck, looking out to sea . . . and that her hat was fastened with a white cockade.

But her hope of her husband's honour was vain. He never did join her on the continent after his release and, save for a slur cast on her good name by rumour-mongers or by Broughton's enemies, Margaret Murray was never heard of in her home parts again. In time her husband presumed her dead.

Of Murray himself, it is difficult to know whether a later confrontation with Charles Edward, over his defection, or the vicious rumour from Rome that Margaret had become the Prince's mistress, brought him the greater pain. He can have had little peace of mind in those years for he had lost everything, wife, honour, friends and much of his fortune. But perhaps for the sake of the fervent times when he was a loyal kindred spirit to the young Chevalier, one can allow him the contentment they said he had with the young English Quaker girl who passed in after years as Lady Broughton.

THE FLITTING OF
OLAV THE FAIRHEAD

You can hear the same tales on different islands, sworn by natives of each to belong to them alone. But travelling-men, selling their goods or their music, and exchanging stories and ballads for food and shelter, took myths from place to place, embroidering them and confusing them . . . maybe making of them another tangle of the isles. Take the legend of the flitting of Olav the Norseman. Three islands claim it, but in folklore the place matters less than the tale. There are details of name and date in this story that do not fit history, but the legend flourishes and there's no doubt a nub of truth whenever . . . wherever, it took place.

It belongs to the days when the Vikings still occupied much of the rugged west coast of Scotland and their proud chiefs held, as vassals, men whose ancestors had owned those lands for centuries.

Lachlan Mhor was one such puppet, hereditary lord of a string of islands and shorelands around Mull and Coll. Born to occupation he had never known any other way of managing his territories except beneath the command of an overlord. Perhaps because he had never been an independent chief he did not chafe unduly under the domination of the Norse Lord, Olav the Fairhead, but dutifully did the rounds of his islands to see that his people had enough food and adequate shelter and also to collect the heavy dues in fish and small crops that Olav demanded of them. The people grumbled but, like Lachlan, had never known any other way of life or lived without occupying strangers. Some would have had their Scottish lord do as other island chiefs had done and rise against the Norse, but most were happy enough to welcome Lachlan when he came, and to listen to his haunting voice singing to them as they gathered round their peat fires.

For Lachlan Mhor was more minstrel than warrior and took delight in singing the old ballads, and telling the sagas that belonged to the days long before the Vikings came. Those songs and legends, the playing of his little clarsach and the pleasure he took in sailing the sounds and firths in fine weather, may perhaps have been a consolation that Lachlan scarcely knew he needed in his unproud position under Olav.

Life might have continued so until his three score and ten years if he had wooed and won a Coll or a Mull or a Treshnish island girl . . . a girl who would have been happy with his gentle poetry, and whose father was content with the way things were under the Norsemen. But one summertime Lachlan's voyaging up the western seas took him to Barra where on a curve of sand he met a girl, a beautiful girl wandering along the water's edge with the wind in her long hair. The sun sparkled on the shore and shone on clumps of pink thrift. Above her, sea-mews cried forlornly, and the romantic heart of Lachlan Mhor was lost. Flora, in her turn, was much taken with the tall island lord who had appeared out of the shimmer of sun on sea and who spoke with so soft and musical a voice.

He told her he was chief of his people, under Olav the Fair, in islands to the south. She told him she was Flora, daughter of the Macleod Himself of Harris and that from there she had come on a visit to her aunt on Barra. They roamed the rest of the day away, she listened to him telling the faraway tales of his island forefathers, in days before men knew of other islands and the great mainland. She spoke of the old Hebridean legends and of her strong warrior father. It was nearly a week before Lachlan Mhor left Barra to sail on to Tiree. By then he had won from her the promise that if her father gave his blessing they would be wed before the winter solstice.

But The Macleod had heard of the tall minstrel lord of the southern islands, who had no stomach for battle, and he compared the young man ill with his hero-father. There were no Viking overlords in Macleod's domain and he despised other chiefs who tolerated being underlings. He was a proud man, but he was also shrewd, he accepted in his heart that the Norsemen were now grafted on to the other western isles and well-nigh impossible to shift. If there were chiefs not willing to rise against them then perhaps it were better to make blood ties with the Norse themselves and consolidate, than face eternal raiding from Viking ships. Accordingly when Lachlan made the long journey to Harris to ask for Flora's hand he was met with scorn.

'Never, Lachlan Mhor! No daughter of Macleod of Harris goes wife to a song-singer that honours his clarsach above his battle axe. A chief's daughter mates with a real chief and not a makar. Flora will marry with Olav the Fairhead for he has made himself true chief of your lands.' And he stalked away with his attendant, not waiting to listen to any protest from the poet-chief. Lachlan was thoughtful and crestfallen as he returned to his ship. Flora loved him. She had told him so, but maybe her father was right and he was not fit husband and protector for a daughter of The Macleod.

When he was troubled Lachlan neither wrung his hands nor vented temper. He sang. And as he sailed home for that day he lifted his voice on the sea wind in sad dirges of lost love, and when he had sung all of those that he knew, he went on to the ballad-sagas about mighty warriors of long ago. Two or three of those tales of great leaders he sang and wished he were one of them, valiant and adventuring to make his lady proud. Then, still some miles from home, he stopped singing suddenly. What kind of man was he, to lose his love to a tyrant overlord, who had come like a pirate from his own country . . . and do nothing about it but *sing?* He went to the ship's prow and looked over the grey shrugging sea, silent, as he never had been silent before among his men. Olav Fairhead would not have Flora!

Olav lived, with a small household of men, in a keep set on a wide flat rock in the small loch on one of Lachlan's islands. There was no wife there yet, but Olav would find women for his men from the surrounding lands. He himself would marry Flora and found a dynasty here among these pleasant Scottish islands. Unofficially he held this and two others and had plans to carry his conquests much further. In the Viking tradition the true chief was the man of strength. He had never seen Lachlan Mhor for his home was on another island and it was their stewards who did business together. But he knew Lachlan for a man of straw and it would trouble Olav not at all to sweep him aside and others like him, sail round those islands and declare them, not simply occupied land, but his own by right of conquest.

Lachlan made for the island where Olav had his stronghold and for two days wandered the shore round the lochan observing the keep where the Norseman held court with the forty men who kept the native Scots in thrall. He noted which walls were blind, studied the outlook tower and the entrances, all the while keeping himself out of sight of anyone who might be on the watch. He went to an old seer woman who could tell things from sky and star, and knew the old Norse sagas even better than Lachlan knew his own. It was something of their many celebrations that he wanted to hear.

'Come the solstice there'll be feasting all night long with Olav and his household . . . if the carousing's good they'll celebrate till dawn,' she told him.

Lachlan bore his soul in patience until the night of the solstice and with a party of his own men came to the island and stole down to the lochan shore. They had their weapons but Lachlan left his with the others and, carrying only the little harp, walked openly across the rough causeway to the grass knoll of the inner island. Already he could hear the sounds of laughter and revelry. They had seen him and his clarsach from the look-out and the strong-door was opening to him amid cries of welcome . . . for was this not some wandering music man come to entertain them?

Lachlan played and sang to them as he had never played before. He sang the ballad tunes of his own people but with words telling instead of the triumphs and glories of the Norse, of their heroic deeds and the swiftness of their long ships. He made them happy and proud. And they drank to that. Even the look-outs were among them now, drawn down to the hall from their posts by the haunting music. He gave them slower, sadder ballads of lost loves and families across the sea . . . forlorn echoes of their old life. And they drank to that. He quickened his rhythms and played for their own circle-dances, their contests of footwork, and of leaping, laden with arms and shields, over the great hall fire. And they drank and drank to all of that.

Then they began to be less agile, less inclined to contest and fling. Some lay sprawled and ready to sleep. He paused and began to pluck out the simple tunes their mothers used back home to cradle them. Now the music was soothing, lulling them, the night was almost past and one by one they all slept, so that Lachlan was the only man left awake in the hall.

He laid aside his harp and, moving quickly among the sleeping Norsemen, disarmed them all, walked quietly several times to the doorway, out on to the causeway and threw each axe, sword and broad-dagger out into the loch. Then he rippled a chord on the clarsach.

That was a signal to the men on the shore. They rushed the causeway, the sound of footsteps rousing the Norsemen to defend themselves. They scrambled to their feet looking for their weapons, someone brought other daggers from the weapon store. But it was too late. The battle was short and swift. The Norsemen decimated, their island keep taken, their chief's life at the mercy of the Scots, Olav was ready to parley.

It was agreed that in return for his life and freedom, the Viking lord would forego his hopes of Flora and return to his home among the fiords, taking with him such men as would not now swear fealty to Lachlan.

When word reached Flora and her father on Harris that Lachlan had used his despised songs and harping to outwit the great Olav, the old warrior thought again about what it was that made a man a man. And Flora, trembling to think what might have befallen Lachlan on his island exploit, decided that, while she had been proud of him as a warrior, she would find it easier and more entertaining to live with him as a minstrel.

A few days later she stood with her father watching as the long-ship passed Harris, bearing Olav Fairhead towards the northeast and his own land. Behind, to escort him out of Scottish waters, came Lachlan in his own ship. And by the time the Norsemen were off the north coast, Lachlan had leapt ashore on Harris to claim Flora as his bride.

It was long years afterwards when Lachlan Mhor had been laid to rest with his harp, when his sons and grandsons were grown men and strong chiefs, that the battle of Largs finally returned to the

Scots their western isles and coastlands. But the sweeping out of Vikings like Olav from small islands one by one was the forerunner of that memorable day, and in time coming, there was every year a revelry in the island stronghold from which Olav had tyrannised over crofter and fisherman. And in Lachlan's lifetime he would sing the new song-stories of the skirmish on the lochan island telling the sons of Flora of their history.

THE MASTER OF
THE GOOD SHIP CLITUS

There were four calamities that changed the life of Betsy Miller. Before them in the early 1800s she and her young sister were being reared in the town of Saltcoats by a gentle mother who had lady-like accomplishments of her own, and a happy knack of passing them on without friction to her daughters. They were not people of great wealth; rather what the townspeople called 'bien'. But Betsy played the pianoforte nicely, made correct afternoon calls, arranged flowers pleasingly and showed the young maid Nellie how a proper table should be set with snow white cloth and the modest silver from their sideboard. When need arose too she could chide her young sister Hannah into the same seemly ways.

A small matter that did concern their mother was that, from time to time, the douce Betsy would seize a thibbet apron and a scrubbing brush and get down on her genteel knees to help little Nellie get her work done for the afternoon. Or Betsy had been known to plunge her white hands into a tub of wash-suds when she came on the maid heching and peching with weariness.

'Betsy, Betsy! Best mind Henry doesnae come and find you darging like a skivvy. He'd no' like it.'

'More fool Henry,' said Betsy cheerfully. 'A man should be glad o' a wife that's no' afraid to work.' But she knew in her heart that Henry would be glad of no such thing.

Betsy was to marry Henry Porter and her mother allowed herself some small satisfaction that her daughter would make a fitting match for Henry, son of a prosperous Irvine merchant, and that she had raised her girl well able to be mistress of his gracious home in the better part of town.

When Betsy's father, the master of the sailing-ship *Clitus* was home from sea with his son, and saw his fine-mannered lass setting about the back yard with a broom, he threw back his great bearded head and laughed at her spirit. And his wife thanked her stars that she, and not he, had the upbringing of their daughters and that such goings-on on Betsy's part were only an occasional aberration.

Life for the Millers was ordered, pleasant and held pleasures ahead for a tasteful unostentatious wedding, the home of a young matron daughter to visit, the coming surely of grandbairns, and the certainty of respect, bordering on envy, among their peers.

Then the first calamity struck when Mistress Miller ailed suddenly and, before her bonnet for Betsy's wedding was chosen, had died and been laid to rest in the old kirkyard.

The second calamity was revealed within days of the funeral with an auditing examination of the accounts of Betsy's father. He had always been more of a seaman than a business man and that was exactly what the books disclosed.

'It's just that bit cargo I lost to the storm in the winter there, and that I've more creditors than debts owed me,' argued Captain Miller lamely.

'Bankrupt!' said the lawyer.

The third blow came when the Captain was still reeling from the first two. His son, whom he had left in Antwerp to conclude some business with a regular client there, had seen the way the wind was blowing for his father's business. He wrote now that he had spoken for the Antwerp merchant's daughter, and was even now drawing in his chair under their solid and expensive table and would not be back to Saltcoats. The talk in the town was that he had drowned and the family let the tale stand, for good name's sake.

Now Captain Miller was back from the lawyer's office with the tell-tale books in his arms.

'So you see, Betsy lass, the upshot of it a' is that I've taken oot a big mortgage on the hoose here,' he explained shamefacedly to Betsy, who was now responsible for running their home and would have to know what was what.

'How big?' demanded Betsy.

'Seven hunner pound.'

It was worse than she had steeled herself to hear.

'If only your brother . . .' he began.

'Never heed my brother,' said Betsy firmly. She pulled off her cuffs, pushed up her sleeves, lifted the ledgers out of his arms and opened them on the table.

Two hours later she called on Henry. Loose tongues had informed the town of the Millers' affairs and he was already displeased that his prospective gude-father was in a disreputable financial position. Now he was frankly appalled when Betsy told him she would be taking to do with the running of her faither's business from home.

'I think I cannae let my wife dabble in a man's world o' work like that Betsy. Captain Miller'll just hae to keep his own heid above water,' he said, in the tone of a man who had just delivered a final decision. Betsy bridled. Her father's head was two-thirds below water now and Henry's choice of words had been unfortunate against a man whose last cargo was at the bottom of the sea.

'Aye . . . the running of my faither's business, *and* forbye that,' she said sharply, 'I'm thinkin' to go wi' him on his next trip out, to see just what's what wi' his kind of work when he's at sea. So it's maybe best we forget weddings and such for the present, Henry.'

She left a half-angry, half-relieved Henry. That idea of going to sea had been an impulsive response to his pique and had not entered Betsy's coppery head until that moment, but she smiled and began to relish it with each step as she marched home.

Miss Miller astonished her dressmaker next day by ordering two serge skirts, four thick cotton shirts and shawls that she could tie round her back, out of the way of her arms.

She left Nellie and young Hannah to the care of each other and the oversight of her father's lawyer, and two weeks later left the polite society of Saltcoats fluttering with the clash that Betsy Miller's wedding to Henry Porter was postponed and that she had gone on board the *Clitus* like any of the town's apprentice-seaman lads.

Betsy found herself to be a good sailor and revelled in that first voyage of discovery. She learned something of shipboard life and its work jargon and she found the meetings with merchants on the continent and their talk of cargoes and bills of sale, fascinating. She took a second trip, met other customers and learned to judge a good stack of timber.

She was young and resilient and, having seen the 'away' part of the business, felt ready to work at home as her father's junior partner and resume her former pleasant life. There would be some lean times ahead until they were out of debt, but they would ride out the storm.

But the fourth calamity had still to happen. Although Betsy's spirits were high, her father had been more seriously rocked by events than his bluff manner suggested. Wife, son and good name . . . all gone, and now these altered prospects for his daughters. At the end of that second voyage, just as *Clitus* sailed into harbour, Captain Miller slumped over the wheel, dead of heart failure.

Betsy brought him in and, by the end of that week, had arranged his funeral, collected payment for their cargo and been to the bank to pay off the first fifty pounds of her father's debt.

On the way home she saw Henry across the street, handling a dainty young lady into a carriage with great care, and a great load she had not known she carried, slipped off her shoulders. She turned and went down to the harbour, took a deep breath of sea air and cast a proud look over her father's ship.

By the end of another week she had released Henry from any lingering obligation and signed herself up master and registered owner of the sailing ship *Clitus*. She had visited three building companies and two shipbuilders in Saltcoats and Ardrossan, and taken home small orders for timber, given half in mirth at the girl merchant, half out of sympathy for the family's plight.

The crew was a little doubtful, but they had liked Betsy's direct, eager-to-learn manner on board and were amused at the novelty in prospect of sailing under a lady-master in her twenties. They all agreed to serve her.

Young Hannah had a smeddum to match her sister's and was managing well and thriftily at home with Nellie for company. And so with a high but wary heart Betsy Miller set sail again, in sole command of the good ship *Clitus*.

Betsy was not foolish. She had much to learn and, while she expected to be obeyed, she relied greatly on the older salts sailing with her, to advise and, if necessary, overrule her judgement. England, Ireland, France and the Low Countries were her beat. She learned the seafaring terms of spars and riggings, masthead, mizzen and mainsail. She studied navigation by sextant and star, charting, signalling and the stowing of cargo, and she learned to recognise the need for tar and oakum. She had her own duties and turns at the helm and took no more than a minimum of sleep so that she could ask the whys and wherefores from the seamen on the watches.

When she came ashore next time she paid off another bill for fifty pounds.

In time, as well as carrying the timber, she added wines to her hold, and spices that had come from the East through France, and she began to exchange coal for limestone between Ireland and Ardrossan. For her own quarters aboard she had the first poop ever built on a ship of the *Clitus* class and made a trig little home there, leaving the crew as much as possible to their own male camaraderie.

In five years her father's debts were cleared and in seven there was a comfortable little nest-egg in the Miller account. When Nellie married, Hannah tried life on board too, but she didn't revel in it as Betsy did, and after that was content to play her part ashore.

If Betsy ever regretted Henry she kept that to herself. When she was about twenty-nine, a passenger boarded the ship late one night when she was abed and next morning the man had asked to see the master, to say a word of thanks for his hospitality. His astonishment at the sight of the snowy mutch-cap surrounding the winsome face which appeared from the poop, had the sailors chortling. The stranger was intrigued.

Not until Betsy was but a memory in those parts and past caring, did any of her loyal crew ever let dab that, after that, the lean tanned Norwegian timber merchant travelled regularly on the *Clitus*, that he talked and laughed and dined with her . . . whatever else . . . during the twenty-two years that Betsy captained her ship. For even when her petal cheeks had put on instead a ruddy glow she was a jaunty, merry woman, and a good companion.

It may be that she reversed the normal ways of menfolk masters, living the single life when she was at home in Saltcoats, and enjoying conjugal-type comfort when she was at sea. She called Lars Olsen her 'first mate' though what precisely she meant by that only the pair of them ever knew.

THE HEIRS OF THE DUKE OF DOUGLAS

When Archibald, 1st Duke of Douglas, died in July 1761 he left his kinfolk in a rare old tizzy. He had been too fond of the good life to settle early to domesticity, and prime-life was on him before the need for an heir really hit him.

Archibald had a sister, Jane Douglas, with whom he shared memories of a happy childhood; but the two had become somewhat estranged, while he pursued his pleasures at home and she spent much time travelling on the continent with her husband and a lady companion. There was a slight taint of Jacobite sympathy about the little party which made a stay away from Scotland seem prudent, for the time being.

Apart from his sister, Archibald's nearest relatives were the Duke of Hamilton and his family, several cousinships distant.

Archibald, now in his fifties, had already begun to regret not having married, when word came that Jane, at the age of fifty herself, had produced twin sons during a stay in Paris. He took heart . . . perhaps irked a little at his sister's presumption in calling the first-born of her boys 'Archibald' after him.

'It's maybe in her mind already that wi' my name-tag on him he's my certain heir,' he remarked to a dining-companion, shortly after hearing news of the birth.

'An' is he no?' queried the friend.

Archibald was roused now, by this confirmation of his sister's view, that he was written off as able to father a lad. He thought on Jane and the genes he shared with her. Maybe the Douglases were built for middle-aged parenthood. His father and grandfather hadn't been young men when the last of their children had been born.

Intent on being upsides with his sister, Archibald left the drinking and gaming to his friends, and embarked on the swift wooing of a far-out cousin, Margaret Douglas. He enjoyed the chase and the resulting marriage, for Margaret was a delicious creature, who adorned his home and greatly enlivened his declining years. She bemused, tantalised and delighted him. But she did not bear him a child.

Duke Archibald took to his last illness philosophically. It was a pity there was no son, but he wouldn't have exchanged those years with Margaret for a dozen sons of a different mother. Besides, there was his surviving young nephew, who had some time ago taken his surname as well as his Christian one, and was now 'Archibald Douglas', soon surely to enter into his inheritance. The old man enjoyed a last frail walk in his walled garden where the herbs were sweet and marguerites splashed white against stone walls. He died in July 1761.

By that time Lady Jane's other twin son had died, young Archibald was thirteen, and the field seemed clear for the boy's parents to step in and have his claim made and confirmed, as rightful heir to his uncle's wealth and estates.

But there was another small boy with at least one of his guardians just as zealous for his rights as young Archibald's parents were for his. There were those distant relatives, the Hamilton family, and in particular the new little three-year-old Duke of Hamilton, James George who, although at a few removes from the deceased Duke Archibald of Douglas, would have been his heir had there been no nephew.

James George of Hamilton had several guardians, but the young bead-eyed Lawyer Andrew Stuart, more than the others, was a shrewd man, intent on his baby ward's best interests. Andrew Stuart found himself very curious about that fortuitous birth, far away in Paris, of two sons to Lady Jane. Not one boy, but two, a double chance at their uncle's estate, lest one should fall to a plague.

'Is it no' a strange-kind thing that the Duke o' Douglas's sister Jane gets to fifty wi' nae bairns and then, of a sudden gets the twa lads?' he remarked to James George Hamilton's young mother (considering her youth and beauty oddly called the Dowager Duchess). The Duchess shrugged slim shoulders. She thought it quaint enough that her three-year-old toddler was Duke of Hamilton, and found it hard to consider that he might also be lord of the wide Douglas lands in Lanarkshire. Besides she had already on her mind a second notable marriage for herself to the great Duke of Argyll, and had no room in it for any other weighty consideration. She took Lawyer Andrew's remark as no more than a passing observation.

'She's a fine strong woman Jane Douglas, and the lad's there to be seen. He's no' just an imagination. There's been bairns afore now to mothers that age.'

'How many d'you ken like that yoursel'?' asked Andrew.

She picked a flower and handed it to him, thinking about herself in the grand Argyll castle at Inveraray. 'None, that I can mind,' she said.

Andrew Stuart had been named guardian by the late Duke of Hamilton and he was a man to follow his duty wherever it led him.

It led him first, shortly after that conversation in the garden, to Lady Jane's own account of her travels, of having lived at several different addresses during her stay in Paris in the summer of 1748, and of being delivered of her twins by a Madame La Brunne in her house in a certain Rue, in Paris. It led him next to Paris itself. There, his spare scholar figure curved like a bow, he prowled round pensions and district offices spending several gratifying weeks playing detective and following one or two fascinating lines of enquiry.

If the lawyer drew blanks at the addresses Lady Jane had given as having been hers in Paris, blanks were exactly what he wanted to find. There appeared to have been no midwife, Madame La Brunne, at the house named as hers (though there had at various times been one or two of different names). There had, it seemed, been no births of twin boys there thirteen years before . . . nothing to suggest that the Madame had ever actually existed. Searches in newspaper offices, *arrondissement* documents and police records did however tell the Scots terrier that in July 1748 twin boys had been abducted from a Paris household and never recovered.

Armed with his findings an exultant Andrew Stuart came home to advise the Hamilton family that, on little Duke James George's behalf, there should be a contesting of Archibald Douglas's claim to his 'uncle's' estate.

'All these tales about the lad's birth to a woman old enough to be his grandmother was a tissue o' lies . . . and worse, Ma'am!' he reported to James's mother. 'For there's the taking away of the twa French bairns.'

With the advice of Andrew Stuart and on those grounds a counter claim to the old Duke of Douglas's estates was prepared for the Court of Session.

It took four and a half years for the case to come before the Edinburgh court, a hearing by fifteen eminent lawyers.

Andrew Stuart was a persuasive man and was offering substantial evidence. The verdict was given in his favour for the now eight-year-old Duke of Hamilton. But . . . only by casting vote for, before that was cast, seven were for him and seven against. Enough to encourage the Archibald Douglas faction to take up an appeal to the House of Lords, asserting that their boy was indeed true-blood nephew to the late Duke.

Pride, integrity, pique and dignity all surfaced now and the antagonisms between the two sides became bitter far beyond the normal rivalries of litigation. The opposing lawyers grew testy and irritable and one made the mistake of referring to the touchy Andrew as a 'mean commoner'. Now Stuart was a far-out sprig of the Royal House and considered himself decidedly more aristocratic, higher-born, than the man who had miscalled him. He hoped too that time would discover him to be also the better lawyer. Nerves were taut on both sides over the pending appeal, and the cut and thrust of the courtroom became a reality when Andrew Stuart called out his opponent. The challenge was taken up and a duel with pistol and sword arranged in London. The two met in Hyde Park with their gentlemen. They were perhaps better with sparring words than with weapons, for both discharged their pistols harmlessly, and reached next for their swords. But their uneasy seconds intervened and persuaded them that honour was already surely satisfied.

The parties had to bear their souls in patience for eighteen months altogether, between first hearing in Edinburgh and the appeal in London. The battalions were big on both sides but, in the end, the earlier judgement was reversed and the claim of Archibald Douglas was substantiated, a welcome coming-of-age present to the young man whose origins had been made to seem so obscure.

Who can tell whether it was ever any compensation to Andrew Stuart that Archibald, French or Scottish, became a responsible and well-loved laird, living ripely to the age of seventy-nine?

Perhaps those who tell this tale admired Andrew Stuart too much to believe that he might have been mistaken in his conclusions about his adventures in Paris. And perhaps he himself overlooked the possibility that, only two years after Culloden, a Jacobite family might have made a number of wary moves of residence in Paris, enough to confuse even themselves, concerned as they must have been about the double pregnancy of the middle-aged Jane. Maybe, after thirteen years in a different country, memories were not easy to unravel. And perhaps Andrew did not understand that it might have been difficult to remember the exact name of a midwife who had briefly attended the family so long ago. As for the stolen twins, Paris was a teeming city where such enormities happened often enough in those pre-revolution days, and there was certainly no sure evidence to connect the crime with Lady Jane and her husband. Whatever the truth, seven of the fifteen at the first hearing rejected his evidence, and finally so too did the House of Lords itself.

Andrew Stuart was a disappointed man and there must have been those who reckoned that, apart from a very adequate fee, he had won nothing from his endeavours. But in fact he had gained in two ways. His professional standing was set for life by this Douglas cause-célèbre, as an indefatigable fighter and clear-thinking lawyer, and his name had been brought before the public spectacularly through the duel. A second bonus was the taste it had given him for genealogical searching into similar cases of controversial inheritance. He burrowed with happy obsession equally into the births, both sides of the blanket, of minor notables and the highest in the land, most colourfully perhaps in the long-disputed legitimacy of the Stewarts to have been Kings of Scotland.

Although they have no real bearing on this story, there were a few ironies in its wake which round off the matter interestingly. A sting in the tale for one who spent so much time and energy teasing out birth mysteries and trying to keep lines of ancestry unsullied, was the 'marriage' of his own younger brother (who had acted as his second in the Hyde Park duel). For James Stuart, serving in India, had married a high caste princess in a Hindu ceremony. Andrew could not bring himself to believe that James was truly wed, or to acknowledge the small niece who came to live in Scotland and might have sweetened his later years.

Another little twist came about when Andrew Stuart eventually took his disputatious talents to the House of Commons, where he sat for ten years as the Member for Lanarkshire, graciously supported by the lord of those parts, Archibald Douglas, whose claimed origins in Paris, quarter of a century before, he had been so anxious to expose as fraud.

THE BIG DEOCH AND DORIUS

Mistress Eezie Abercorn, the ale-house wife, was a nippy wee woman with beady eyes, not much loved around the near end of Forfar where she lived. Even the oldest inhabitant had never seen her laugh or smile or even pass the time of day, friendly like, to anyone. She was a sour-puss that the bairns ran from when they saw her coming. Indeed it was well-known about the town that Mistress Abercorn was happy only when she was involved in small litigation of some kind and that was a gloomy-enough happiness even when she was winning her case. And win she always did, for she had a knack of being right, that fair irked her neighbours. She took every quibble that she was sure to win, to the Bailie Caird who, although a genial well-thought-of chiel was, like herself, an honest stickler for the letter of the law. Between them they had quite a record of successes which pleased her more than it did the Bailie. There had been the neighbour whose dyke was rebuilt for a stretch of ten yards, six inches into Eezie's kail-patch ground; there was the small boy who fished a length of the burn touching her land and landed his father a heavy fine; and there was the old woman who made a pie of apples hanging over her fence from Mistress Abercorn's tree. In all of these the reluctant but meticulous Bailie was obliged to find in her favour.

So disputatious and dour was Eezie that her ale-house premises might have been shunned by thirsty townsmen if it had not been that her home-brewed ale was far and away the best for six miles all ways round Forfar.

Another of her less endearing ways was that she was ever on the look-out for the least offence to give her an opportunity of going to law. And one autumn day, when the Michaelmas daisies were making a fine splash at her doorway, just such a chance arose.

Eezie had spent the morning brewing her ale-malt then set the browse in a tub at her door to cool into the nectar that was so popular with her clients. She bustled back inside to tidy up and to draw up a nebby new notice for her drinking parlour, minding her clients not to do this, that, or another thing.

While she was thus occupied at the back of the cot, her farmer neighbour, Benjie Cattenach, was passing the front, leading in his two-three cows for milking. He was making towards his yard unaware for the moment that the cow at the tail of his tiny herd, Primrose, had sniffered the air curiously outside Eezie's cot and, greatly drawn by the mellow, fruity smell from the tub had lumbered aside from the slow plod home and begun to taste the browse. She lapped carefully at first and then with increasingly abandoned pleasure, and much wet noise. But Mistress Abercorn and Benjie Cattenach were too engrossed to hear or see, yet, what Primrose was up to.

It was, as ever, a fine strong brew and Primrose but a novice drinker, so that by the time Eezie came out to the door to take in her ale, she not only found the tub very empty but the culprit very fou. Poor Primrose was staggering and dancing and rolling her soft brown eyes, like a two-man dressed-up cow Eezie had once seen at a fair. Primrose crossed and recrossed her shauchly legs trying to get one to each corner to hold her up while, inside her stomachs, the ale swished and sloshed and made her glow. Mistress Abercorn was furious. She took a switch to the cow's rump making her roar and lurch worse than ever, and bringing Benjie Cattenach running back to see what was amiss.

'Amiss! Your beast's made awa' wi' all my yill, that I'd set here to ripen. That'll cost you a bonnie bawbee Benjie Cattenach. See the pot's tim. I'll thank you for the full price o' the tubful.'

The normally easy going farmer had been angered to see the wallop coming down on his cow's back and wasn't for giving in so easy.

'Bide a wee, Mistress. You'll no' get a penny off me that way. Gin you'd've putten your pot at your back entry, you'd still have had it whole and hearty. You cannae blame the coo.'

'Aye, can I no'? We'll best hear what Bailie Caird's got to say about that. Twenty years I've been puttin' that tub at this door, why should I think the day to put it to the back — just because you've a drunken coo?'

And she flounced inside banging the empty tub as she went, determined to go again to law; while Benjie took the reeling cow home, wondering as he went just what her milk would do to the Forfar bairns next day.

As she had promised, Mistress Abercorn in her best plaid, was at the Bailie at the stroke of eight next morning. She told her tale, righteously indignant, and it was all Bailie Caird could do not to laugh aloud.

'Aye well, Mistress. You've right enough had a sore loss and you're likely due a bit recompense.'

'The full cost, Master Caird, sir, and half as much again for my trouble!' insisted Eezie.

'I canna gie you judgement yet, wi'oot I hear what Cattenach has to say. Come back the morrow and I'll let you hae my decision.'

If Eezie had been a poor wee soul scrabbling for a bare living instead of the contentious woman that she was, or if Benjie Cattenach hadn't been a good friend of the Bailie, Mistress Abercorn might have notched up yet another legal victory. But, as it was, the Bailie wracked his brain for a way to give the ale-wife a come-uppance for once instead. He went to see Benjie.

'What's this then, aboot your coo that's ta'en to the drink?' Benjie laughed.

'Och, I was fair put out yesterday at her whippin' the beast, but I best just pay up and keep her douce.'

'Na, na, man. It's past time Mistress Abercorn learned there's losin' a case as well as winnin' one. She's comin' to see me at noon the morrow. You be there an' all.'

When the three assembled next day Bailie Caird sat them down in front of his table and gravely cleared his throat.

'Now Mistress . . . you put your yill to cool at the door, eh?'

'As I do day and daily, John Caird.'

'And after you'd been ben the hoose awhile, you came back and found what?'

'That gomeril o' a coo, her legs a'ways, swayin' and dancin', drunk wi' my browse.'

'But still on her feet?'

'Aye, whatever that matters. I didnae take her in and set a table to her, if that's what you mean.'

'Och, it matters, Mistress . . . and you an ale-house wife! Tell me this Eezie Abercorn. Gin a traveller comes by on his horse or even a-walking, and chaps your door for refreshment, wi'oot he wants to come inside. What do you do then?'

'That doesnae happen, Bailie, for my cot's on the road to nowhere . . . all my folks sits in to drink.'

'But what would you do?' he persisted.

'Sell him it there . . . an his siller was good.'

'Weel you'd be agin the law, Mistress. D'you no' ken the old law that says when a traveller comes by on foot or on his horse and doesna sit down to it, you've to gie him his stirrup-cup, his deoch and dorius, wi'oot he pays a bawbee . . . for the hospitality of the place. Noo it seems to me that the coo Primrose was but a traveller seeking a deoch an dorius fae you, for you say she drank her yill, on the hoof. So go you home Eezie Abercorn and mind how you're to treat wi' travellers . . . or else Bailie Morrish and myself'll hae to take away the papers that gie's you the right to brew your ale.'

It was a nine days' wonder in Forfar that Eezie Abercorn had lost a case at last . . . and to a cow at that! She sulked for a week and then Benjie Cattenach came by one day when she was picking the last of the purple daisies. He put his hand in his pocket.

'Here, Mistress Abercorn . . . a tub o' yill's a lot to lose, and for the pleasure it gie'd my Primrose I think I maun pay you for it.'

Folk seldom spoke kindly to the prickly Eezie. She flushed . . . and took the coins.

'Weel . . .' she began with an effort. 'Best I get you your deoch and dorius while you bide here.' And she hurried inside and brought him back the cup.

After that he was often to be seen having his stirrup cup outside the ale-house, until folk who knew about the Bailie's judgement of Solomon, shook their heads and began to wonder whatever was going to come of it all.

Until well into his prime time of life the world of the man they called Big Jon McKim was bounded by the forge at his croft cottage, by the hamlet and the three thorn trees of Carlingwark, by the Stewartry of Kirkcudbright and, by the girdling hills of Galloway. There he lived with his seven sons and his gossip-targe of a wife, Meg; far from the great world of politics, court shennanigans and the rebellions surrounding the young Stewart King, James II.

It was true that it was the Douglas family with wide lands in Galloway, which was at the heart of those far-off rebellions . . . the Douglases, who would so dearly have loved to sit on James's throne. But word about their machinations came to the likes of Jon McKim only as tales of adventure long miles away, and the burly smith and his friends saw the local tyrannies of their Douglas lords as much greater sins than those intrigues in Edinburgh and Stirling.

Threave Castle was the Douglas stronghold in Galloway and its present master was William the 8th Earl, whose path towards power was littered with the bodies of those who stood between him and the overthrow of the King. But it was his heavy hand on the country folk round Threave that riled them to impotent fury. There were his demands on them for bond labour, tillage and multure, there was his relentless throwing into vagrancy of men who could not meet them and, worst of all, there was, it was whispered, his taking at will of their womenfolk for his passing pleasure.

As well as the rent of his forge and small croft, McKim's dues to his lord were to see to the shoeing of the Douglas horses and to render general smithing services in all manner of iron work at Threave Castle. The only pleasure red-powed Jon McKim took in his visits to the Castle, on its green sward island in the River Dee, were in his craft-work well done and in the occasional glimpses he had there of the lovely Lady Douglas, a Margaret like his own termagent at home, but a million miles away in soft voice and gentleness. It was a matter of wonder to McKim that such a lady could endure her vicious man.

The peasant people smouldered quietly enough, applauding secretly when they heard rumour that the King had annexed Douglas lands in other airts, but resigned to their lot at Earl William's hands here in Galloway.

But matters came to open anger when the political plotting and murder spilled real blood into their own backyard.

Earl William had two allies in his struggle against the King and together the three family heads could more than match James in numbers of armed men and in wealth to pay and equip them. From their joint position of strength the three could snap their fingers at loyalty. But they wanted a fourth, a man in the King's favour who could intrigue for them at court. Their choice fell on another Galloway man, young Patrick MacLellan, the Tutor of Bombie near Kirkcudbright. Earl William expected Sir Patrick to jump to his demand and was incensed when the man refused.

'Think you you've no duty to your laird in Galloway?' stormed William.

'I'm more minded on my duty to King James, my Lord.'

'His royal days are no' for long, Patrick MacLellan. There's sturdier men better fit to rule than James Stewart.'

'Gin that's so, William Douglas, they'll hae no need o' my right hand.'

Within days the young man was in Threave dungeon, his own keep gutted and roofless.

The King sent the Captain of his Guard to Threave with a royal warrant for the safe release of Patrick MacLellan. For answer, the messenger was shown the headless body of the Tutor of Bombie; and himself threatened with hanging like a tassel from the Castle gallows knob.

James Stewart may have been only three-and-twenty in the year 1452, and King of a small country, but when he heard of the murder of Patrick MacLellan his wrath was like that of an outraged Emperor of half the world. And knots of plain folk round Threave told each other in hushed tones that James had summoned their Earl to Stirling, under safe conduct of the Great Seal.

When William reached the Castle there and was bidden to dine, he may have thought that James had not yet heard of the Tutor's death or else that the young King was trembling for fear of the mighty Douglas tribe. Whether he had much appetite for dinner is not part of ancient lore . . . a pity if he did not enjoy the meal, for it was his last. When it was over King asked Earl to make penance and to give him, there and then, a vow of future loyalty. When the proud William bridled and hedged, James, never heeding Great Seal and safe conduct, daggered him on the spot and had the Captain of his Guard 'mak siccar' with an axe.

Down in the south-west at Carlingwark, with Jon McKim and his friends, there was wary relief that their tyrant would not be back to oppress them . . . wary because his brother, James, who would be the 9th Earl, was a shadowy unknown who might turn out to match William for villainy.

At first Earl James seemed less murderous and wilful than his brother, and appeared to be content with sniping skirmishes and small floutings of the King's authority. But he was only biding his time, for he was just as ambitious to overthrow the Stewarts; and had the added staw against the King for the killing of his brother. Soon he was threatening neighbouring landlords *into* unholy alliance with the Douglas faction and *out of* loyalty to the Crown. A smoking ruin of a castle left here, the firing of a crop there, the reiving of cattle over the hill, the unpredicatable, vindictive harassment of the countryside . . . that was Earl James's way, and in time the restless destruction and plunder became as disruptive in Galloway as the more spectacular deeds of the last Earl had been. There was no peace around Threave and as well as the lesser nobles that he killed, the herds and labourers, the millers and cot crofters, were just as much his victims of that restless time.

But the King was losing patience altogether with the troublesome Douglases. One by one their keeps and estates in other parts of Scotland were confiscated to the Crown, and the day came when word arrived in Galloway that time was running out for Threave, their sturdiest stronghold.

Luke Ghyll, the travelling mole-catcher came twice a year to the countryside round Carlingwark, and it was he who brought the news that there was a King's force on its way to the south-west.

Like the other menfolk, Jon McKim and his sons listened with interest to the moudie-man.

'The King's himself's w' th' army and brings great cannons. He bids to pound the Douglas out o' Threave. He'll no' catch Earl James himsel', they say, for he's about his other affairs, up Stirling or Edinburgh way.'

If Jon McKim spared a thought then for the gentle Lady Margaret at the Castle, it was with a sad shake of the head that she had brought this danger on herself, by the folly of taking for second husband her first man's brother and becoming châtelaine to the 9th Earl after what was surely a grim life with the 8th. His own garrulous Meg tushed and toshed at her foolishness and had no doubt of the righteousness of the King's justice. Encouraged by her certainty, the smith began to look forward to spectating at the battering of Threave.

And that was all the part Big Jon McKim expected to play in the drama.

Luke Ghyll was gone by the time the King's troop arrived in Galloway but his intelligence had been correct and James himself was indeed at its head. This was King come to People with a flourish of banner and drum, and the backwaters round Carlingwark Loch hummed with excitement. When the army set up camp at the Three Thorns hamlet beside the forge, Jon and Meg McKim were centre-stage.

From there King James could look across to where Threave Castle rose from the island in the Dee and plan the assault on its nine-foot walls. He deployed his bombards and opened fire.

But day after day the cannon balls struck dully against the staunch Threave walls and fell harmlessly to grass and river below. And there had been other spies and news-carriers besides Luke Ghyll, so that the Castle was well-stocked with food, and with ammunition for its thousand soldiers to snipe back at the army indefinitely. Different bases and angles were tried for the casting of balls, but Threave had been built a century earlier by an unpopular lord to withstand insurrection by his people, or just such a seige as this. It stood firm now as it had stood then . . . and King James II was frustrated and angry.

He pondered in the nearby abbey where he had made his living quarters, and as he tramped, hunch-shouldered along where the willows wept into the Dee, he eyed the mighty curtain-wall of Threave and at last went home to his abbey room and called his counsellors.

Some say that then the King sent to Linlithgow, to his own armourers there, for a heavy new cannon; but Jon McKim, his sons, and all the generations who have lived round Carlingwark since those days, knew better. They knew that it was to the little Three Thorns forge that James came for his great Bombard.

A party of captains and engineers, and three gunners whom McKim was to get to know well, Dand Aitken, Rab Howerd and John Ker, sat late into the night with the smith, and from the very next day such an organising and scheming went ahead as had never before been seen or heard of, in those parts. Look-outs from Threave saw to-ing and fro-ing, coming and going, in-ing and out-ing of men busying themselves across the Dee. The McKims pored over plans and drawings with the engineer-armourers, and spent hours with the gunners Dand and Rab and John, until Mistress Meg screamed that there was neither cup nor sup left in her larder.

There was a great digging of earth, hammering and shaping of stone, as Jon McKim and his sons tore out their small forge. In its place they built one that would have housed five horses, and with a chimley wide as the smith himself was high. Neighbours lent their strength, eager to be caught up in the King's great enterprise.

Then the MacLellan family, still smarting from the beheading of their honest Tutor Patrick, called on every household to bring to McKim a bar of iron, and on the forester to provide a tree, twenty inches wide and as long as two tall men. The forge fire roared and the straight iron bars with hoops to gird them, were wrapped white-hot round the tree trunk until they were welded tight and the wood could be burned away. The base was made and, as the cannon was finally assembled and the gun tilted to forty-five degrees, villagers and crofters came to the forge to admire the results of their labours. They clapped horny hands on the body and gaped into its huge maw.

'Look-you at her muckle great mooth . . . like my ain Meg's,' chuckled McKim, glancing round sheepishly to see that she was safely clashing with the other women, well out of earshot. And the name 'Meg' stuck to the Three Thorns bombard.

Meantime stone chips flew on Benan Hill as men there gouged out granite to make cannon balls, heavy as Galloway cows, to match the 'Meg'.

Dour and determined, the King inspected his artillery, consulted with his experts, considered Knockcannon summit, Glenlocher hill and Benan itself, for the least obstructed line towards the Threave curtain. He made his choice and the six tons of bombard, and its ammunition, were hauled to the site.

It has been whispered for centuries since that exciting time, that it was not only the bombardment that tolled the ultimate knell for the Douglas garrison. For there was something else afoot round the gates of Threave. There were unusual night sailings of small boats to and from the island and much confidential chatter in small ale-cots along the banks of the Dee. The Earl was from home and even if he had tried to winkle himself back inside the Castle again, the besiegers would have been alert to take him. He had left his stronghold to faithful stewards and custodians . . . or thought he had. Promises of land and gold were being offered and accepted at those night-time on-goings, with great bribes to important men and more meagre ones dwindling down the ranks of the Castle defenders. And now the scene was set for the second stage of the siege.

At the hour when the Earl's family was dining, three cannon balls were hurled by the 'Meg', the Castle was breached beside a window slit, and it was all over with no more resistance.

Jon McKim had a pang when report came out of Threave that the ball crashing from his bombard into the refectory, had taken with it the white hand of the Lady Margaret and the wine cup that it held.

And it was only much later that he came to terms with his part in that incident . . . when years after, it was said that the gown with its long sleeves elegantly pointed below the wrist that was the new fashion-rage in high places, was copied from the cut of Lady Douglas's dress, specially designed to hide her infirmity and allow her to enjoy the social round.

There were other compensations too, of course, when the power of the Douglases was broken. The countryside round Carlingwark thrived more peacefully under new lairds, among them the blacksmith. For he had his reward of the King, in the granting to him and his heirs, of the land of Mons, or Mollans in Kirkcudbright. It is not recorded what Meg McKim had to say when the bombard from her man's forge, with its yawning mou, became a legend in the land and was known ever after as Meg of Mollans or Mons Meg.

Note: There is much evidence for and against the truth of this story of the constructing of the cannon Mons Meg in the Stewartry of Kirkcudbright; but whether it was built there or at Linlithgow (or even Flanders as some say) its subsequent history is well-documented. Three centuries after the siege of Threave, Cromwell took it to London as a spoil of war.

A hundred and fifty years later, Sir Walter Scott, then in high favour with George IV, urged the King to have it returned to Scotland. It came, was dragged up to Edinburgh Castle in a skirl and whirl of pipes and banners, and, except for a recent brief return to London for examination, restoration and repair, it has sat there in honoured and admired retirement ever since.

In times long before continents, countries and islands were placed and measured in a mesh of latitudes and longitudes there was a single curved triangle of land at the edge of the world. It lay like a sickle moon beyond Scotland, its creamy white shores washed by the North Atlantic, the whole great island sheltering Skye and the mainland coast from fierce Arctic winds. Those who lived there were hardy from exposure to wild weather and had to be dourly energetic to survive, with only small crop farming and the cattle they grazed on its machairs. The island was therefore a happy-hunting-ground for the strong sailor-men of the Nordlands who came looking for slaves and cattle, and even peats, to carry home as prizes. It seemed worth the hazards of the journey along the north coast, to turn the corner at Cape Wrath and plunder this New Moon island. The Nordic giants were warriors, men more of strength and endurance than of imagination. And so, many generations passed before one among their Chiefmen, a man they called Leod Spadebeard, pondered over a better idea he had had, than venture the tempests along Pentland time after time, for a few captive islanders, a load of peats and two or three head of cattle.

The plan had come to him, clear as clear, on a day when a push from his foot dislodged a solid-looking rock on his own home shoreland.

'Would it not be wiser and craftier,' thought Leod, 'rather than come back and forth and waste time pillaging the New Moon island, to tow it home whole, anchor it in my home fjord and take my plunders as I need them?'

It seemed so sensible that it was a wonder that neither he, nor any other, had thought of such a plain idea before.

Leod Spadebeard was a thorough and careful planner and it was no time after the thought had struck him that he sought out a fjord sea-woman and asked her how he could find the best and strongest tow rope to pull the great island home. For a mermaid surely knew that the salt sea would weaken and rot ordinary rope. Her long hair swirled round her in a golden coil as she drew a slim hand down its length, and considered. Then she spoke.

'Here is what you should use. You must gather the hair of many maidens and twist it with great care. It will make a strong rope that the sea will not seep into and perish. Never yet have I seen hair that rotted in the water.'

There was a cold breath on Leod as she turned quickly away, then only a dark, deep swelk in the sea where she had been.

Spadebeard had a busy time in the west before the next equinox, raking the crescent island for maidens. He carried them in sobbing, wailing bevies to his longship, and there gave each a long razor shell to shave the head of another and, when exhaustion with their crying left silence for Leod's voice, he tried to soothe them.

'You will go free when your hair lies in a pile at my feet. When every head among you is shorn, I will take you back to your homes.'

They raged and complained and one sulky, defiant maid uttered a dreadful curse on her dark mane as she cut it. But the rest hacked away at the hair in resentful obedience and at last, weeping and clinging to each other for comfort at the frightful sight of their tufted heads, they were rowed back to the white shore and allowed to scramble home to their stricken families.

For three days Leod and his men stretched and pleated, twisted and tested the gleaming maiden-hair rope, and then in the black silence of a moonless night they sailed in towards the Eye of Lewis, threaded the rope through it and secured island to ship. Then his men took up their long oars again, dipped them slowly and rhythmically into the sea and inch by inch began the long, heavy haul of the crescent-island towards home.

At first it slid sweetly through the water on the silken tow rope and when the Viking men had gone perhaps a mile, they allowed themselves a cheer at the capture of so rich a booty. Then a strand or two of the hair caught on a rugged hill, and another on a crag. The longship jolted slightly and Leod tried to caw the rope loose.

But there was another shudder and the Norsemen watched with horror as the island began to crack open and break up. First, the part the islanders called Barra floated off, then the Uists . . . and Benbecula . . . and a dozen small rocky islets formed in the wake of Lewis as it was pulled jerkily away.

Back on what was now a scatter of smaller land-masses, there was uproar as the people were rocked and thrown about. Only the maid who had called a curse on her hair was calm.

On the galley-ship Leod could only watch with rage and disappointment that only part of his plunder was still attached. He pulled again on the rope as if he could add his own strength to the rowing power. But his horror deepened and a hoarse growl came from his throat as the length of hair that the sulky maid had cursed, tore slowly apart strand by strand . . . and then came the final break. The thrust of it pitched Leod headlong into the sea and he went down, down forever into its icy depths.

Shocked and sobered, and far from cheering now, the remaining men trailed, not the island, but only the broken rope. They made for home as fast as the grey shrugging waves would allow them, with nothing to show for glory and the fine dream, but the tail of maidens' hair. And further and further behind them the base of the curve of land settled calmly on to the sea bed again, but broken for ever into the scattered crescent of beautiful islands their people began to call . . . The Hebrides.

GLOSSARY

Ackvity whisky
an if

Bachle, bauchle old shoe
bawbee halfpenny
billy chap, fellow
birk birch
braws best clothes
bree cooking liquid
bunnet cap

Cadger carter
callant young boy
caller fresh
canny cautious
ceilidh concert
chap knock
chiel fellow
clay clay pipe
cleck gossip
colpindach young cow
craws hooks
cubbie Orkney basket

Deave deafen, bore
deoch-an-dorius stirrup-cup
douce sedate
dover doze
drouth thirst
dwam daze
dwyn decline
dyke wall, fence

Fae from

fankle tangle
feel fool
fey otherworldly
flyte scold
forby, forbye also

Gangrel vagrant, itinerant
galravaitch romp
gauger exciseman
genzie jersey
gin if
giorgio non-gipsy
glammer bewitch
gomeril blockhead
gringe grit the teeth

Haar mist off the sea
heuk hook, sickle
hidlins secretly
high-falutin fancy (of talk or behaviour)
hinny endearment, honey
hobbledehoy ill-mannered youth
hullarackit noisy, romping
humplock small hill
hurdies thighs

Jink dodge
jouk dodge

Kail vegetable
keep castle
kenspeckle wellknown, noticeable
kist chest

Leet list
lief (as lief) as willingly
loup jump, skip

Machair sandy tract by the sea
makar poet
malison malediction
marchpane marzipan
maudlin drunkenly sentimental
mort-kist coffin
master-hoosel master
of ceremonies
mou mouth
moudie mole
multure toll payable in meal to
miller or landlord

Nebby nippy
neep turnip

Orra loon odd-job-boy

Pech pant
pottish potash
pow head

Quine girl

Rant roar, shout
reiver rustler
rig farming strip
rock and distaff spinning
implements

Scart scratch
shauchly shambling
shilpit puny
siccar sure

skeely skilful
sleevin skinny
smeddum energy, will-power
smit infection
snell cold, sharp
sough moan (of wind)
spaewife fortune-teller
spiel discourse, tale
spier ask
spuuk matchstick
staw aversion
steep soak
stoup drinking vessel
swee swinging rod over fire
for cooking
swelk whirlpool

Tak' tent pay attention
tate small amount
thibbet coarse cloth
thirl bind
thole endure
thon yon, that
thrawn obstinate
tim empty
tocher dowry
tot add, fill up
tulzie tussle

Usque whisky

Wheen large quantity
wight strong man

Yett gate
yill ale
yirdfast halfburied